Sexual Suicide

Norlita Brown

Author Aaron Bebo contributed work to Conversation 4. His work was printed with expressed permission from Story Ta Tale Publishing.

Sonya Wynn, Alicia Jones, Laura Hodges, Cynthia Hodges, Rachel Anderson and Shunda Staples-Ray contributed work to the conversations. Their work was printed with their permission.

Cover design by André Foster of Niche Creative Studio

Photography by Solo Impressions Sherryl 'Solo' Boyd

Screen shots by SSRAY Films Michael Motley

BROWN ESSENCE, INC.
P.O. BOX 82462
CONYERS, GA 30013

Please visit our website at brownessence.com and let us know what you think.

DEDICATION

This book I dedicate to the women whose excitement of my first novel, *Somebody Else's Vows*, caused this sequel to come into existence quicker than I anticipated. Thank you so much for your positive feedback and your motivation.

Diane Wall

Rachel Anderson

Antoinette Copeland and

Ebony Smith Brown

ACKNOWLEDGING:

God for guiding me and allowing me to see the manifestation of my.

ROLE CALL PLEASE:

My darling, darling baby, Clinton Sanford Brown! Woo hoo, God has blessed me with a wonderful and beautiful husband. You're my chocolate drop!

Ve'Lynncia Jazzemin Morgan and De'Vray C. Rogers, I thank God for blessing me with you two, my handfuls. Ebony Farrow, I pray that our relationship moves past misunderstandings. I work so that my children's children can be blessed, so this is for you Javion Robertson for stealing grandma's heart, Xazavioer Farrow for being so full of life and making me so proud of your tiny 4 years, X'zyon Farrow, you truly bring new meaning to bundle of joy, and Baby Moses, X'zeven Farrow – so absolutely adorable you are.

You have seen them before, and they're here again because these ladies are my world, I love them so much, I thank my big sister almighty Sonya Wynn, my adorable baby sister Alicia Jones, my sister-cousins Laura Johnson and Cyn'thia Hodges who were very valuable with their input.

Todd Tyler, thank you from the bottom of my heart for all the encouragement as well as the proofreading of my work. So blessed to know you.

If you haven't seen the book trailer please stop by and check it out. It definitely helps bring these characters to life. So to that I must thank Shunda Staples-Ray, the director, a woman who is blessed and highly favored, thank you for putting together an excellent production team and cast. Landry Zuck for his work as cinematographer, editor and director, Erick Guy Toby and Michael Motley for their work on the production team. **Jules Nobles** took on the character of Alyssa and made it her own, so genuine, professional and excellent at her craft, **Tony Franklin** as Quan (Q) was just so handsome we had to give him the role and he did such a wonderful job; **Brandon Alston** as Ahmad, the eye candy; **Danni Clay** came in and rolled up her sleeves as she took on many hats, photographer, make-up artist, actress, and model – she fit the lovely Tee in so many ways; **Cedric Lewis** as Carnell, please don't sleep on him, he is an excellent actor; **Myletta Lacy** as Jayla – she performed so well, I forgot she was acting, **Courtney Lane Maki** who learned her lines so well under time constraints, everyone was impressed; and **Allie Brown** as Barbie/Tiffany;

Shelia Terry, your support has been so phenomenal. It is wonderful knowing you. Your food is off the chain too. Looking forward to having you cater again.

Dr. A'ndrea Wilson from my heart to yours, thank you.

M-PACT – Let's do this!

Words cannot express the gratitude that I have for all of you who have purchased our work, the compliments have been so well received and we thank you for that. Special thanks to Shirley Allen, Sheila Cook, Michael Grimes, Ron and Blondie Knuckles and Tyrone Ferguson.

Sexual Suicide

You gave me something that
I never asked you for
I in turn gave him something
he wasn't ready for.
To my surprise and
rather to hers,
he gave to her,
what I had given to him
I tried to explain
I had gotten it from you,
and you said
you had gotten it from her
But she didn't know
 that she had given it to you.
Therefore,
it seems in this sexual merry go round,
 we tend to keep passing around
The leading form of genocide
Sexual Suicide...
till death do we part!
-    Pure

ON MY KNEES...

with my face smashed as far in his lap as my throat would allow me to go, pleasuring him in a way that I would rarely indulge my husband with. Yet, it was causing an exciting energy to flow through my body. I was happy, if only for the chance to touch his body again, to feel him inside me in some form. I tugged at his pajama pants that he wouldn't let go of.

"Stop," Ahmad said denying me the pleasure of a full view.

"Why not?" I asked as I released his manhood from my lips.

"You already said that you were not having sex, so I don't need to take my clothes off."

I was puzzled by the comment, we were having sex, albeit oral sex, but sex all the same. I didn't want to let go of the intense passion that I felt being so close to him. So I settled for what he gave me, I took his shaft in my hand and finished what I started. His moans were making my heart race. My excitement grew.

He grabbed my arms and pulled me away from him. I wondered what I had done wrong. I knew the fact that I rarely performed the act was probably showing in my performance. I tried hard to hide it, with my tongue, my movements and gyrations, so why did he pull me away. Just as the thoughts made their way through my mind, he pulled me close and kissed my lips gentle and soft, then harder. It felt like he needed me more than he needed any other woman.

"I have to feel you, Alyssa," he said. I was at a loss for words, in fact, I don't think neither of us needed to say anymore. He led me back to his room. I threw my clothes quickly to the floor, and stared back at him. My senses came to me. What was I doing? Q was at the house waiting for me.

"Ahmad," I said with a heavy breath.

"Shhh," he said and kissed my lips gently, the hardness of his body pressed against the softness of mine, all cares went out the window. "I've got it right here," he said as he held up the condom.

TIME HAD DECIDED...

not to be my friend. I knew Q was clocking my every moment, waiting on the opportunity to pounce, with his "aha!" Q had filed for divorce several months ago and had I not contested it, we would be happily single right now. That would have been a whole lot better than these feelings of guilt racing through my veins. I don't know why I contested it either.

If I were to guess, I would say it had everything to do with the fact that Q didn't just leave it at we had irreconcilable differences. No! He wanted to cry on the judges shoulders talking about how wrong I had done him. To make matters worse, he brought up the fact that I had fallen in love with Ahmad. I would have tried to argue my point but instead I decided to play hardball. Chrisette Michelle's *Blame it on me* couldn't counsel me then. I couldn't help but laugh as I recollected the events of that day.

"Your honor," I said as the tears filled my eye lids. I tugged at my brown vest, then brought my hands to my face and wiped away the tears with all the drama I could muster, "I am so in love with Q." I looked over at him and watched as his jaw dropped. "I don't know why he wants to leave me," I said and took hold of the

9

Kleenex that was being offered by the bailiff, I wiped my nose and continued. "I feel like I am the only one who has put any effort into saving this marriage and now he's decided to just throw me out like yesterday's trash." I sat back down in my seat as if the weight of it all was just too much for me to bear.

"We have built so much together and if only for that reason we should give one another a fair chance to work beyond our differences."

Judge Michaels looked at me as if she wanted to cry with me, as if my pain was hers and countless other women's. She looked at Q, "Mr. Robertson, I tend to agree with Alyssa," she said. I took note of how she referred to me informally even though this was the first time we had ever encountered one another while Q received the harsh tone reserved for a child being disciplined.

She picked up a pen and began writing, "I am going to recommend that you guys seek counseling," she said, "I am assigning you Dr. Carol Donovan," she continued before tearing a sheet from her pad and handing it to the bailiff, who in turn handed it to Q. "You're more than welcome to seek your own counselor as well, but this one is not an option."

She stared us both in the eyes as if we were being parented for some wrong we had done, "I want to see you both back here in 6 months, but I want you to give it an honest try. Okay," she said as she looked directly at Q.

I left with a smirk on my face knowing that all of it was just a game. I no longer wanted Q as I could tell that he sure in hell didn't want me either.

None of that mattered right now as I drove home from Ahmad's worried that Q would know exactly where I was and what I had done. I wondered what Tee would do in this same situation and then I smiled, today, I was going to try to fill Tee's shoes.

I flew up the back stairs like I had wings, my clothes hit the floor before my feet had a chance to gain steady ground. I jumped in the bed with Q and for the second time that day my head was in a man's lap. I looked up at Q's startled expression, but as I continued to place my warm tongue along everything that was his, I watched him relax and give in to the pleasure.

I tried to force Q to sex me the way that Ahmad just had. I wanted the aggression the passion, but Q just reverted back to our same ordinary sex. I closed my eyes and envisioned the love I had just made with Ahmad, the way his soft lips touched my body, the hardness of his chest, the memories set me on fire and caused my body to explode.

I opened my eyes and looked at Q's boastful expression. 'Humph,' I thought, 'if only you knew, that orgasm didn't have anything to do with you.' I held my tongue and my peace and went to shower with the revelation that my sex life was about to look up.

He Smiled Weakly....

at Tiffany as she sat at the table going over all the details of the wedding. Although they had yet to set a date, she was bubbling with anticipation. Books were scattered across the table, pages opened to cake designs, color schemes and all sorts of wedding paraphernalia.

"Q," she said smiling widely, "don't you just love it! Everything is going to be so beautiful. I can't wait."

He on the other hand could. He sat on the chaise silently watching her. With every minute that passed he was slowly slipping away. His heart was no longer excited to marry Tiffany. He suspected it was because he reacted out of a different emotion. He was angry at Alyssa and felt it was time for him to make some concrete decisions in his life. So he proposed to Tiffany.

It was a decision he was starting to regret. Q wasn't sure that he ever wanted to marry again. Maybe when the six months was over he would just enjoy being single again. Take life one day at a time. It wasn't that she was a bad woman. Tiffany was beautiful and loving. She would cook a hearty meal for him every evening he was home, which was more than he could say that Alyssa would do.

Alyssa made it a point the moment they started dating that she didn't and wouldn't cook. 'Me and the kitchen aren't friends,' she would constantly say every time he came home without the aroma of fried chicken and collard greens or even a simple spaghetti dinner. Alyssa had her days when she would cook. It would always be hit or miss with her. Sometimes it would be the best meal he had ever tasted, other times it would either be too bland or too heavy on the seasonings.

He never complained though. If it was on point, he would clear his plate. If not, well he would simply put it in the microwave and let her know he would eat it later. Of course, later never came. He smiled at the way he and Alyssa had a silent communication that was better than the one they had aloud.

Tiffany walked over and sat on his lap. He actually hated when she did this, but he never told her because he knew that she loved it. So he placed his drink down on the side table and scooped her in his arms.

"What are you so deep in thought about?" she asked as she kissed him on the forehead.

"You know me; I like my quiet time, just to think about nothing in particular."

"Oh, am I disturbing your quiet time, Q?" she shouted loudly, and then she smiled.

"No," he said not wanting her to know that she was actually getting under his skin. He kissed her on the cheek. "So, did you find anything good over there?" He asked nodding in the direction of the table where she left her huge pile of mess.

"Actually, I did but I want you to help me, Q. This is our wedding."

"I told you I don't get into stuff like that, just show me what you like and I'll let you know if I'm feeling it or not."

"Q," she whined "you know they say third time's a charm. So, maybe you should do things differently with this wedding then you did with the other two so you and I can have a beautiful wedding and even better marriage."

"Okay, but not right now."

"I knew you loved me," she said as she kissed him on the nose. "So, what would you like for dinner? I am going to run to the grocery store real quick." Tiffany got up from his lap and headed to the table and picked up her purse and keys.

"Whatever you make is fine, baby." Q said as he walked over to her and kissed her softly on the lips.

"Okay, be back in a minute."

The moment she walked out the door, Q gathered all the books and magazines that she left scattered across the table and put them on the bookshelf. He wiped the table clean, put the chairs back in their place. Then he made him a fresh drink before resuming his place back on the chaise. He clicked the remote and let the soft sounds of jazz fill the space.

He leaned his head back and enjoyed the moment as he wondered where his home away from home would be next. Tiffany had stolen his private moments, his tranquil thoughts and all that gave him peace. This place was designed for his time away from women. Unfortunately, after their engagement, Tiffany had all but moved in.

His sanity was starting to slip away from him, slowly. He took another sip of his drink before closing his eyes. He resigned to use this time to enjoy his peace rather than let his mind replay what he deemed to be his injustices.

DR. DONOVAN AND I WERE...

waiting patiently on Q to show up for our marriage counseling. The sessions were tiring and very draining. They were also giving me another reason why it would have been easier, if not better to have just signed the divorce papers Q handed me, rather than make a fuss about it.

Arms and legs crossed, I rocked my leg, impatiently. It was very apparent that this was the last place that I thought was making good use of my time.

"Wasn't this your idea?" Dr. Donovan asked stirring me from my thoughts. I wasn't prepared for her to speak until Q arrived.

"Excuse me."

"The marriage counseling, I mean I know I was directly appointed by Judge Michaels, but if I recollect my notes correctly, you were the one who didn't want the divorce. Am I right?"

"Something like that." I said trying to correct my posture. I didn't need her going back to Judge Michaels with anything unsavory about me. If she knew that I had given her a performance she may make the settlement lean heavily in Q's favor.

"I don't understand."

17

"I love Q and I want our marriage to work, but the more that I think of everything that we have put one another through, the more I question whether or not it's worth it."

"Have you expressed your concerns to your husband?"

"Not in so many words, but I think my actions have been screaming them."

Q walked into the office, wearing a light grey pant suit with fitted jacket, a dark grey fitted v neck completed his ensemble. His chest was outlined nicely and I adjusted my position again. He was very easy on the eye.

"Mr. Robertson, thank you for joining us. I was beginning to wonder if you would make it."

"I'm sorry, Doc. I got held up on a run. I didn't make it back in town until about an hour and a half ago. Of course, I had to clean myself up for you ladies." Q smiled, Dr. Donovan did too, but I wasn't giving him the satisfaction and I didn't care how sexy he looked right now.

"Okay, shall we get started?"

"I've been ready, if everyone respected the other's time, we would have already started."

"Alyssa."

"Yes, Mrs. Robertson, can we start on a more positive note."

"I don't know that we can, what do you think, Q?"

"I think that we are here because you wanted us to be, so if anyone is not respecting someone's time it's you. If you want this over and done with then you should have signed the papers. Now bid your time and do it correctly."

"Oh so now you want to man up. Any other time you leave me to wear the pants."

"Okay, let's explore that issue for a moment, Mrs. Robertson. Why do you feel you were left to wear the pants?"

"I'd like to know the answer to that one myself, because if you asked me, you weren't left to wear them, you just refused to give them up."

"Really, Q? Are you going to take it there? Let's think back on the time when we were at the airport."

"Damn it, Alyssa, would you let that rest already."

"No, let's not" I said as I turned toward Dr. Donovan to dish my dirt to a paid listener. "So we're at the airport and Q's in line when all of a sudden this white dude comes up and steps in front of Q. Q didn't say a word, so I had to."

"I didn't say anything because the situation wasn't that serious. It wasn't necessary, Alyssa. You keep allowing your Detroit mentality to make you more aggressive than you need to be."

"Whatever," I said as I turned back to Dr. Donovan to finish my story. "As I was saying, I had given him ample opportunity to speak   up   for   himself,   but   he   didn't. So, I said something and told the dude that he needed to back up, because there was a line. He told me that he was already standing there and that he wasn't moving. I called him the liar that he was and when the teller asked for the next person, I went ahead of him and told Q to come on. Well needless to say, the dude called me out of my name. Called me a female dog in front of my 'man'" I said as I put up the air quotes emphasizing to her and Q that I was using that term loosely.

"I looked at Q to respond which he didn't, so I promptly got in the man's face and told him to say it again and see if I don't knock his teeth out of his mouth. He backed up, of course I went after him a little more because he didn't apologize, but I got my point across clearly."

"Okay, I can see how that situation would anger you. Mr. Robertson, why did you not feel it was necessary to defend her honor?"

"Did you hear her? She has it all under control."

"Oh, but Dr. Donovan, I didn't even tell you the best part. When we were finished with the teller, Q told me and I quote, I can't take you anywhere. Is that not icing on the cake?" I was feeling pretty good about myself now and pleased that Dr. Donovan seemed to understand my point.

"Mrs. Robertson, when did all of this take place?"

"Exactly," Q cut in. "This was at least three or four years ago."

"Why do you feel that you are harboring old issues?" Dr. Donovan asked with pen and paper in hand, waiting on my response so she could jot down my every word.

I pursed my lips wondering how the tables turned so quickly. I was so confident that this was headed in my favor.

"I don't think I'm harboring ill feelings exactly," I said as I looked at Q. "I think that what I am doing is keeping record of the actions until Q finally shows me that he is willing to be that man."

"What man is that?"

"Good question, Doc. Keep 'em coming."

"The kind of man that makes me feel protected. I want to feel like if anyone or anything ever goes wrong, he's got my back. I want him to be a communicator, a lover, a friend. I need him to be so much that he refuses to be."

"Okay, that's a start. You have stated what he isn't now tell me what he is?"

"He's an excellent support system. Anything that I dare to do, he's there for me. Any job that I want to walk away from or walk toward, he supports me a hundred percent, which includes financially. I'm comfortable with Q because he doesn't judge me. If I want to be silly and act a fool or serious and have an educated conversation, he floats with me."

"He makes me smile, but most importantly he makes my heart smile."

Q nodded as he listened intently and suddenly I felt that maybe there was a chance for us.

"All of these things are great starts. What I need for you guys to do is take these things home, talk them over. See if the lists get longer or shorter. Q, provide your list to Alyssa, just as she has done for you here today and I'll see you guys next time."

"That's it?" Q asked sounding as surprised as I was that our session had ended so abruptly when we were just scratching the surface.

"Well, Mr. Robertson," Dr. Donovan began as she took the glasses from her face and folded them neatly across her lap. "You do realize the sessions are only forty-five minutes, therefore your late arrival put us behind some, because your wife was here on time, the clock started when she arrived. Besides, I have another appointment in a few minutes. Although it's too soon to tell, I would say that we've made some wonderful strides today, wouldn't you?"

Q looked at me, I shifted in my seat, trying to remember the last time he had this effect on me. He smiled and bit his lip as if he knew he had me at that moment. "Yeah," he answered Dr. Donovan's lingering question. "Yeah, I would say so."

It was Tee Time...

with a slight exception, Tee wasn't there. It turned out not to be the same because neither Bree nor Danni showed this time and Tee was in rare form. Normally, when she was in the house everyone knew it. Although she was louder than most, it was her presence that made everyone aware that she was around. She has this way about her that stands boldly. Tonight was different, if I had not been staring at her, I would have never known she was there, because in actuality she wasn't.

She held her wine glass in one hand while her finger traced the top mindlessly. She lay back on the couch with her feet resting on the ottoman, staring at the blank television. I had just put on Ken Ford's latest cd, *Right Now*.

Another rarity for Tee was that she did not come alone. She had brought an old high school friend with her. Although Tee and I knew just about everything about the other, this young lady I had never come across and I was a little leery about her too. Not because I didn't know her, but it was the way she walked into my home as if she owned the world and everything was at her fingertips.

She was model-type beautiful, just like Bree. Her soft hair flowing to just below her shoulders, light-skinned complexion untainted with scars of any type, her eyes were bright and clear. She barely spoke as she perched herself on the couch next to Tee. She was dressed to the nine, stilettos and all, and if I knew brand names like that, I would call it to you. I could not help but think that Tee done brought somebody else to the group to help me feel like I'm underdressed.

Tee came out of her trance, well partially as she just started to speak to no one in particular, "Why is it that we hang on to men who we know are no good for us? I mean down right poisonous? You know the ones that "can't live without you", but as soon as you make them mad, they run every negative thing, that they think about you down in your face. So then you decide to leave the brotha alone, and right before your eyes he is back in your life again.

I smiled; Tee really was in rare form. I was trying to figure out which one of her men had her in a little funk right about now. "Tee, in order for you to answer that question, you have to start at the root. What wrapped you?"

"He was tall and said all the right things at the time. He had a pretty ass smile. To put it simply, he was beautiful."

"And then when he wasn't? I mean, what happens when he's not saying what you want to hear? You hold on to the fact that he looks good?" I asked. I wanted this flushed all the way out, not just for her, but for me. It was time for me to walk away from Ahmad and I knew it, I just wasn't ready to let go.

"Hell yeah," Tee said in excitement and I knew we were on our way to getting Tee back, "and I am not ashamed to admit it either. Let's not forget the other little special things he does," she

24

said as a huge smile crossed her face which confirmed that she was officially back.

"Well, I think," Jayla began and without hesitation my face screwed, I had hoped that it had gone unnoticed, unfortunately, it had not. Jayla cleared her throat while she stared at me hard. "Tee, can I talk to you for a minute?"

"Go head, put it out there," Tee said.

"Uh uh, this ain't for everybody's ears," Jayla said while not taking her eyes off me.

'Whatever,' I thought, 'bourgeoisie, just like I thought'

"It's cool, Tee," I said "we'll wait while you have your side bar with your little friend." Apparently the sarcasm didn't go unnoticed either. Oh well, my bad, like I said I wasn't one for the poker face or the games. Emauri was the only other person in attendance, and she smirked like she knew I was giving Jayla hell.

"Yeah, Tee," Emauri chimed in as she took a sip of her wine, "go head we good."

"Y'all acting like this my chick or something," Tee said coming out of her calm into a frustrated vibe.

"Oh no, don't get it twisted, we're not acting like anything, but your girl, now that's a different story," I said as I looked at Jayla like she was an intrusion.

"Look," Jayla said as she stood and walked toward me, I stood, if something was about to go down, she would not get the best of me because I was in the wrong position. "I'm gone need you to miss me with all that bullshit," she said as she pointed her finger in my direction. "I came over here to have a good time like everybody else, just because I'm light skinned with pretty hair, don't get it twisted, I will fuck you up."

"I doubt that, Mrs. It, coming in here acting like you God's gift to the world, you better back the hell up."

"See, that's part of the problem right there, little girl, when you grow up you will realize we are God's gift, so don't get mad at me cause I recognize who I am."

"I don't have a problem with you recognizing who you are; I do have a problem with you thinking you're better than everyone else."

"Why, cause I'm light skinned and pretty you assume I think that," Jayla was spitting her words fast, my respect for her was growing.

"I will say something one time that I pray you catch, because one thing I hate is repeating myself. I could care less about your complexion or your hair; they have absolutely nothing to do with my opinion of you. Your character, however, does."

"Look," Tee said "y'all motherfuckers are blowing my buzz, now I got to get another glass cause y'all on some bullshit. Squash that petty shit."

"That's your sister," Jayla said, "I came in here as an invited guest and I'm not feeling welcomed at all, Tee. You said she was cool people and I took your word on that."

"She is, she just going through some shit right now and got that misplaced anger."

I thought about what Tee had just said and wondered how much truth was in her words. I didn't feel like I was angry, but she is right, I never treat a guest this way, even if it's something about them that I'm not feeling, I handle myself better than this.

"I'm sorry, Jayla," I said as I put my hand out, "truce. Let's try this thing again." Jayla shook my hand and went back to sit by Tee again.

Emauri let out a laugh, "Well alright, I thought I was gone have to break out the popcorn."

I smiled, "Okay, Jayla what were you going to say about Tee's comment on poisonous men?"

Jayla picked up her wine glass and sipped, eyeing me suspiciously before she began again. "Well, what I started to say was I think we like the challenge. It's something about women that makes us assume that we can make men change, especially if we're good looking and a good woman. Plus, we like that longevity, ain't nobody tryna start over so we just try to make it work."

"Jays," Tee said making Jayla's name jazzy "you are so right, we love longevity. I know I for one can't stand newness. I like the fact that the one I'm with, as bad as the relationship is, already knows me."

"True," Jayla said "and I really think that's most of us especially as we get older. Don't get it twisted, longevity does not mean stale. I feel another problem is more women are lowering their standards and accepting less."

"Girlllll....keep it coming," Tee sang, "you just spoke some truth right there. I definitely want whatever relationship I'm in to stay fresh."

"I tend to wonder if there is a difference between longevity and comfort or do they stand alone? In that I mean, do we love longevity because we are comfortable or does it have more to do with morals? Do we not want to be seen as that one who hops from person to person?" I asked Jayla and Tee who seemed to be the experts on the topic.

"I am one who could care less about what people think or perceive about me," Tee said. "If I am with a man one week and then with another the next, that's my bizzness, this is my life and I do what I do for me not for anybody else. As far as the longevity and comfort, I do believe they are one in the same. I feel like we stay and we don't want to leave because we've been in it for so long and we've been in it for so long because we are comfortable."

"But see," Jayla began as she placed her plate on the ottoman, "that's another issue. The longer we're in relationships it becomes harder to keep it fresh because people get so complacent with one another. So when you try to discuss it with your partner it often starts an argument then pointing fingers at each other. So what do you do? Keep it to yourself to hold down the drama and keep being dissatisfied? Or do you keep faking it until someone cheats or leaves?"

Her words caught me in the throat. A flush of guilt washed across my face as I recognized how much my own life was a reflection of that very thing. Q and I had become complacent and now I had cheated, but was I forced to? Was it inevitable?

"Yeah," Tee said "because that's what will happen if we are not open and honest in our relationships. I believe that if you can't be honest with your man without him trying to dog the shit out of you, I don't think there is any room for a relationship."

"And you know what we haven't considered, Tee is how many men do you think is going to accept the fact that he's not performing or keeping you satisfied? Nine times out of ten he's going to make up some excuse and blame it on the woman."

I decided to stop being petty and join in on the conversation. I still wasn't feeling Jayla too tough but she was definitely bringing strong statements to the table.

"Okay, Jayla," I said with a genuine smile, "I like the way you said that, because men are not going to accept the fact that they are not keeping you satisfied. What is funny is that society keeps thinking that sex is for men and just something women do to keep their man satisfied, but like you said, what about us. Our satisfaction is not just an emotional or mental one, but sexual too."

"Yeah," Tee said as if she was fading back into her dazed state, "but if we do tell them, we have to worry about all that other bullshit. I want a man who can respect what I'm saying without being called all kinds of names just because I have an opinion."

"Exactly," Jayla shouted as she stood like she had just won the *Price Is Right*, then she sat back down just as quickly as she stood, "they shouldn't dog us out, but they don't know how to handle us on certain issues."

"Wait a minute," Emauri said finally coming to life and interjecting her opinion, "I have to stop y'all here, because I mean, we're putting everything on the man, like it's his fault, but we have not once stopped to think about what we're doing. Like the fact that, we as women have low self-esteem and that's why we are afraid if we let that low life of a man go we won't be able to find that one good man."

"Wow Emauri," Tee said, "that is the real of the matter. We do have low self-esteem in some sense. Even the women who people consider beautiful or the women who consider themselves super fine have a problem letting go of a man that is so very wrong for them. It's like we're hypnotized by that third leg."

"Yes," Emauri laughed "I truly think we are hypnotized by the foreign object!"

"Tee," I began, "yes we are addicted to it, but they come a dime a dozen, so what does that man have that the next man doesn't?"

"Hey kid," Tee said as I frowned, it was a habit she had of calling Bree and I kids, I was far from being that. Even though she said it with love, I refused the title, especially in the presence of company on a topic that is clearly for grown folk. "First of all, they don't come a dime a dozen, because I'm sure you have been with a man and thought that he was alright 'he'll get better', then you get another man and he makes you feel like your body is going to explode, so then he becomes addictive because not only is he this way one time, but its every time y'all get down in the bedroom."

"Emauri," Jayla started casually, "I've never thought that we ALL have low self-esteem but, I think that we are just emotional creatures it's just our nature, therefore we take a little more sometimes. I can agree with Tee, that A LOT of beautiful women have low self-esteem because they don't see what others see in them."

"All of the negative things he has said about us starts to sink in our heads and makes us think we are worthless," Emauri said. "That's why we keep letting them come back! Ladies we have to pick up our self-esteem and K.I.M (Keep It Moving). "

"Come on Emauri," I said with an obvious look of disbelief, "now I am with you that many women have low self-esteem, and yes men contribute to that big time, but I also feel that it's a cop out. If a man tells you the sky is black if you see it is blue, who do you believe? Same difference, if you know who you are and the beauty in yourself, both inside and out, then why would you turn around and let a man tell you otherwise?"

"Alyssa, I do believe that men contribute to our self-esteem," Tee said, "but it is so much a cop out like you said. If you can't build yourself up without the help of others then what is your worth? If you can't tell yourself that you're beautiful even on the days that you don't feel it then how can you expect others to see what you can't see yourself?"

"My point exactly," I said. "This has been such an enlightening conversation, but after all that we said, we still haven't answered Tee's question, 'why does it take so long for us to get these poisonous men out of our system?' I evaluated my "bad" men relationships and I can't find one time where I voluntarily walked away. For me, something major had to happen to end the relationship, like him cheating or something else drastic."

"I started acting and treating them like they did me," Emauri confessed. "Eventually, they got enough of it and left and the feeling I got was like the whole world was lifted off my shoulders."

"Okay, Emauri," I said, "I feel your interpretation of reciprocation, but do you think it was easier for you to have them leave you, than for you to just walk away from someone that was destructive in your life?"

"I think it was easier for me to have them leave me because I felt like I had the upper hand when they kept crawling back to me I didn't like to be rejected, I had fun being the one who did the rejecting that way I had control of my life."

"It seems to me that all you really accomplished was helping to boost their ego and self-esteem, by allowing them to be the one who walked away from you. They are not privy to your thoughts so therefore, they can only view the events as they occurred, regardless to how you treated them, in their mind they felt as if they were too good to be treated like that by you, whereas you could have felt that same way and walked away."

"At that time I really didn't care what they thought just as long as they were out of my life."

"Well," Tee began with her own confession, "I haven't gotten rid of the poisonous man in my life. He is still with me, and that's why I brought up the subject because of what I am dealing with. I don't consider myself to have low self-esteem at the moment but I used to. I do think I lower my own self-esteem every now and then by looking at myself and believing that I am not worthy to have a fine man, looking at myself from time to time and saying you're too fat, to have a man as fine as this. Then I snap out of it and realize that I'm just as beautiful as the next woman, the thinner woman. But as far as your situation Emauri, I think that it is better to let that man know where he stands instead of playing games. I think that by you allowing him to walk away under the pretense that he's the one doing the leaving is bullshit. In the relationship that I am in, I have told this dude exactly how I feel about everything he does and says that I don't agree with. After that is said and done, we go our separate ways for a minute but he comes right back, and I let him because of the addictive magic stick."

"This was a real good dose of truth," I said wrapping the conversation up as I looked at my watch. "I like the fact that we have a group of mature adults who can handle truth as well as deliver it. I just hope no one gets sensitive and start taking offense to anything."

"Yes, please don't take offense to anything I have to say," Tee stated with all seriousness, "nothing that I'm saying is a personal attack it's just the way I talk."

"Yeah, you knew I was talking about you. However it would be a tragedy to have a forum such as this holding tongues and biting lips."

He Walked Around....

his apartment with the thought of Alyssa weighing heavily on his mind. He was angry at himself for allowing her to get so close to him. It seemed that everything he tried to keep her at bay somehow brought her closer. It was frustrating. And now that he had felt what it was like to hold her close and be inside her warmth, he couldn't get her off his mind.

Something had to change quick before he found himself being driven to hell. He found himself at the Mosque more frequent, praying on an instant change of events. He didn't know what to do or why this was happening to him. He tried avoiding her. He even threatened to take a restraining order out on her.

With all that he had tried he still failed. He looked to Allah for answers but never understood why Alyssa was constantly on his mind. It seemed that even when they tried to stay apart they would wind up somewhere together. He was beginning to think it was fate, but before he settled on that he would try harder to distance himself from Alyssa. She was beautiful, but she came with a lot of drama that wasn't good for either one of them.

I HELD THE PHONE...

to my ear, puzzled. Why in the world was a White woman calling me from a private line. "This is she?" I said after she asked for me like she and I had been friends for a long time.

"Bitch!" she said before I heard a dial tone.

'Wow, seriously.' I thought as I put the phone back in its cradle. I was a forty year old Black woman who didn't play these types of games when I was a kid, and I refused to play them now. I was, however, curious as to who she was, if for nothing else but to beat her down for disrespecting me. That was something I had not outgrown. I loved a good fight, even at 40, although ever since I got arrested for fighting, I have calmed down quite a bit.

I picked the phone back up and called my big sister almighty, Tee. "Girl, I am so pissed," I started as soon as she picked up the phone.

"Okay, look, you and Bree are going to have to stop that shit."

"What?" I knew very well what she was referring to. Bree and I were both guilty of starting a conversation without a hello, how you doing, or more importantly are you busy right now.

"Don't play with me Alyssa."

"Whatever, Tee. Can I start now?"

"Go head, but don't do that shit no more. I'mma start hanging up on y'all."

"Look who's giving out phone etiquette when you don't follow them either. You never say goodbye, we know the conversation with you is done when we hear the dial tone."

She laughed, I smiled; I felt better. Tee had that effect on me and I was glad she could lighten my mood.

"Okay so anyway, what were you calling about?"

"Oh, right, I just got this phone call and some White girl gone toss the b-word at me and hang up."

"I see you still watching your language huh?"

"One of us has to 'cause you just let yours go any which way and loose."

"So who do you think it is and why you think she's pressing you?"

"I don't know, but when I think harder about it, for some reason Barbie keeps coming to mind."

"Barbie? What the hell?"

"You know old girl from the party awhile back."

"Oh right, Barbie. Why the hell would she be calling you?"

"You said she left with Ahmad right?"

"Yeah, but that was months ago, Alyssa."

"I know, but suppose they still got some things going."

"And that would concern you how?"

"Not necessarily concern me, but concern her because, my next subject of conversation was I had sex with Ahmad the other day."

"You did what?" she nearly screamed in my ear.

"Oh yeah," I said as I licked my teeth and smiled widely, "not only that I pulled a Tee."

"How the hell you pull a Tee?"

"I drove straight home and laid it on Q so hard, all he could do was give in. But get this, Q and I haven't been having good sex in a while, now all of a sudden, it was like BAM! So he pushed his chest all out like he did something."

"Well he did didn't he?"

"I mean he did a little better, but not enough to cause the type of orgasm I had. No, that was all Ahmad."

"Don't tell me you were thinking about Ahmad while you were sexing Q?"

"And you know this! What, what," I sang. I wasn't sure what I was so proud of. All of this was against my morals. Sexing two men in the same year was off limits let alone the same day. Tee was rubbing off on me and I wasn't sure if that was a good or bad thing, but my body was telling me, it was a great thing. "So do you think I'm right?"

"You are what you want to be. I mean, you know I don't give a damn, I do me and don't care who like it. Shit, if I'm in the mood for three men, then that's what the hell I'm gone do."

"Uh Tee," I said as I tried to stifle the laughter that was threatening to escape in convulsions, "I was referring to Barbie." I went to the office and sat at the desk, propping my feet up, something I would never normally do, but I guess I was really feeling myself today.

I watched as a blue Mercedes pulled slowly up in front of my house and parked.

"Who the hell is that?" I said as I placed my feet on the floor where they belonged and sat up straight.

"Who the hell is who?" Tee asked as if she could really answer the question for me.

"Somebody just pulled up in front of my house," I responded giving her the visual that I had.

"Don't start that shit again, Alyssa."

I laughed, when Tee and I were sharing a house in our early twenties, I had convinced her to go outside and tell a bunch of guys that they could not park in front of our house. After they had royally cussed her out and told her that it was government property and they could park there if they so choose, she in turn cussed me out for putting her up to such a foolish feat.

"I'm not, this one just seems a little odd," I said as I got up from my chair and pulled the blind open a little wider for a better view. "Now ain't that some shit!"

"What?" Tee almost screamed in my ear, anticipating some drama.

"Did I not tell you the person that called was Barbie?" I said feeling like I was reciting a line from *Set It Off*.

"Don't tell me ol' girl is in front of your house?" Tee laughed. "Yeah, that's definitely some shit."

"Tee, let me hit you right back," I said as I pushed the end button on the phone before she could respond. I tossed the phone on the stairs and swung the door open. I didn't know if she had come packing or not, and I didn't give a damn. If she wanted blood, then that's what she was going to get.

Unfortunately, I wouldn't get the satisfaction, the second our eyes made contact Barbie stepped on the gas fast leaving tire tracks in the road, but not before being brave enough to throw me the bird. That just pissed me off even more. I ran back in the house and slammed the door shut, raced through the house like a hunter on the move. Hit the kitchen and grabbed my keys, out to the garage door, raised it up and jumped in the car and put it in gear while the garage door was still in motion, praying that this heifer wasn't about to make me cause any damage to my new Infinity in my haste. I had just traded up and the mocha brown paint wasn't even dry yet.

I put the car in gear like I drove for NASCAR, forgetting this was a residential area. My speed matched hers with no tire marks in my path, but hers were clear for me to follow.

When the tracks ended, I paused for a moment trying to think like her the best I could. I jumped on the freeway and headed in the direction of Ahmad's apartment. I had to be pushing 90, I didn't check the speedometer, I was trying to gain my composure and slow my speed, but then I spotted her vehicle. I sped back up and pulled next to it, rolled my window down and cut my eye at her for her to do the same, she wouldn't.

Now I wanted to run her off the freaking road, but my senses got the better of me. I knew that my rampage was not about Ahmad but about principles. Either way, she was taking me way out of my element. I was a lady and I intended to carry myself like one. Her beat down would have to wait for another day. I got off on the next exit and headed back to the house. There was more than one way to skin a cat.

SOMETHING ABOUT HIS VOICE...

still made me weak in the knees. "Hey," I said in my soft kitten tone. It was hard to believe that less than an hour ago I was trying my best to chase down his other lover.

"Alyssa, to what do I owe this surprise call."

"Ahmad, after the other day, do I need a reason to call anymore?"

"Well, usually most people have reasons for calling, and I don't want to sound harsh, but the other day was nothing more than sex."

I bit my lip trying not to let the sting of that reality hit me too hard. His words were harsh and cruel; I was starting to wonder what it was that made me so head over heels for him in the first place.

"Anyways," I said changing my tone to a more hip beat. I couldn't let him know that he hurt me, "I actually did have a reason for calling. I'm wondering how much you're willing to tell me about your girl."

"Who are you talking about Alyssa? And please stop fishing, if you are trying to find out if I am seeing someone else then just keep it real and ask."

"Oh don't get it twisted sweetie, I'm not hiding behind words. I don't care if you're seeing anyone, it was just sex remember." I threw his words back at him, but I knew they didn't have the same effect as they did when they came my way. "Ahmad, where is all of this animosity coming from?" I asked as I backed down from the confrontation we were heading in.

"There is none, I just don't like playing games."

"So," I said slowly, choosing my words carefully hoping not to get the conversation back to a boiling point over pointless issues, "does that mean you think I'm playing games?"

"I don't know what you're doing Alyssa. One minute we're hot the next minute you're on some other shit."

"Here we go with that again. It amazes me how you interpret things, but I'm not trying to keep getting side tracked. I was calling about Barbie."

"And who the hell is Barbie?"

"The girl you left the party with awhile back."

"Are you talking about Tiffany?"

"I guess that's her name, hell if I know. Barbie is just much easier to remember."

"Why are you asking me about her?"

I didn't want to tell him that she was at my spot for fear that he wouldn't give me any information because of it. I really wasn't sure whose side Ahmad was on. This is one of the times that I wish we were a race that kept each other's back at all cost. I decided not to play the games that he obviously was playing and keep it one hundred.

"Take your pick: your girl riding your dick so hard that she calling my house, or the fact that she was bold enough to stop by it. If I'm not mistaken both are valid reasons for a Detroit beat down."

"Oh so now you hood?"

"I'm me! Don't put your labels on me."

Ahmad cleared his throat, and for the first time in this conversation he talked to me like I had some sense, or better yet, like he had some. "Look Alyssa, I haven't been with Tiffany in months. I don't know what her beef is with you but it has nothing to do with me."

I wanted to challenge his statement but my mind reverted back to that night. Q and I had argued over her as well. I remembered the anger in his voice when I called her Barbie after he had already told me her name was Tiffany.

"Yeah, okay," I said softly, I wanted to kick myself for not doing my research first. I had already let Ahmad into my relationship with Q deeper than I had let anyone other than Tee, and now I was painting another unhappy picture for him, as if my having sex with him hadn't painted enough. "I'll talk with you later." The line was dead.

I didn't know if he had hung up before my last statement or after. I was tired of getting caught up in his roller coaster ride.

I wanted to call Tee and vent about my days event since we last spoke, but my energy was on another level. I got up and paced back and forth. I hated letting anything or anyone control my emotions. I grabbed my keys and headed back to my car, I didn't know where I was headed, but I knew that I needed some air to think things through. I needed to do what I often failed to do; have a conversation with God.

IT IS AMAZING...

the things that God shows us when we let go and let Him have complete control. When I got in my car, I tuned into the gospel station and let my heart cry. How I placed myself in situations that held so much drama, was puzzling, to say the least. If I was honest, which I usually am, I would have to admit that a small part of me thrived on the drama. Gave my heart a reason to beat a little faster, let my emotions run wild for a while. Unfortunately, the pain that served as the after effect needed more than a small dose of aspirin.

I didn't expect to drive to Ahmad's house, but that is exactly what I did. It didn't surprise me to see Barbie's car parked outside. My first thought was to go up to Ahmad's house and catch him in his lie. I was pissed. The gospel music that blared through my speakers was partly responsible for me keeping my composure, that and the fact that I wasn't ready to face the truth behind my anger.

I was so heated it felt like smoke was coming from my ears and my nose. I sat in my car allowing my fumes to dissipate. I had already made a wrong move earlier, calling Ahmad about Barbie. I had to think this thing through and make sure I didn't cause myself further embarrassment. Several scenarios played out in my head, I smiled at the one that ended with me beating the shit out of Barbie. That laugh calmed me down a little more.

I flipped open my cell phone and dialed Ahmad. I was cool; there was no need for me to trip.

"Let me guess, you were in the neighborhood so..."

"Oh whatever," I said relieved that I didn't have to fess up to being downstairs. "How do you even know where I am?"

"I saw you pull up, Alyssa. Besides that, I'm starting to know how you do things."

"Meaning?"

"I knew when I hung up from you earlier that I would be seeing you today."

"So what, you have some sort of magical powers, or a mystic ball of some type?" I lay back in my seat and relaxed. I didn't know where Barbie was, but I knew she wasn't with Ahmad. There's no way he would be on the phone with me for this long if she was.

"So are you staying in the car, or you're coming up?"

"Is that an invite?"

"It's whatever you want it to be Alyssa," he said as I watched his door open and Ahmad step to the front of the door with no shirt on. His rip hard abs begging me to touch them.

"Do you ever have on more than pajama pants?"

"Are you going to continue asking a hundred questions, or are you going to act like you came here for a reason?"

I flipped my phone closed and jumped out of the car. My body was already two steps ahead of my mind. Just as I reached the last step to Ahmad's floor, I heard the laughter of a couple coming out of the apartment adjacent to his. My first reaction was to smile at their happiness; my next was to have my jaw hit the floor as I watched Q emerge from the apartment with Barbie nestled at his side.

His next laugh was cut short as he finally took a moment to notice his wife staring at him and his White girl on his arm. His expression matched mine. We were both caught off guard, shocked and no telling what other feelings were brewing beneath the skin.

I looked back at Ahmad for support, the look on his face telling me he knew more than I wanted him to. I wasn't sure who I felt more betrayed by. I looked back at Q, it seemed like time had stood still. His reaction had not changed, although Barbie smirked and moved in closer to Q. I decided I wasn't giving anyone the satisfaction of knowing how I truly felt, especially when I didn't know myself.

"Touché," I said to Q shrugging my shoulder as I reached out and slid my hand across Ahmad's chest. The pleasure of that touch faded fast as I felt the sting of Q's hand across my face. I recognized the sound before my mind registered the fact that Q had just smacked the shit out of me.

Chaos had just erupted. Everyone was always curious if my bark was worse than my bite, well Q was about to find out, cause I don't have time to be selling woof tickets. My fists balled tightly as I turned feeling like Sophia in *The Color Purple*, my body language taking the stance of a heavy weight.

My first aim was going straight for Q's jaw, but the laughter on Barbie's face caught my peripheral, and my punch landed square on her jaw instead. She was so light that it quickly took her off balance. Q grabbed me by the shirt; I smacked him upside the head. He let me go. Ahmad stepped in and it was on.

"Go inside Alyssa," I heard Ahmad yell at me. I was pissed and ready to get it poppin', I wasn't trying to cower inside an apartment. I didn't give a damn whose apartment it was.

"Like hell I will," I said in reply as I did a little jog, my eyes darting back and forth between Q and Barbie, wondering which one of them was going to be stupid enough to make a move.

Ahmad wasn't dumb enough to turn his back on Q so he stepped in the middle, keeping his eye on Q. "Everybody needs to calm down. Alyssa, this is not Detroit, you will find yourself in jail quickly." I stopped my jog and crossed my arms. I started pacing back and forth weighing my options.

"Yeah, okay," I said as I stared Q and Barbie down, "I'll back down, this time. So like I said," I continued as I threw my hands in the air and headed toward Ahmad's apartment, "Tou motherfucking ché!"

"We cool?" I heard Ahmad ask just as I got into his place, I turned to see what their response would be. Q's chest was heaving, he was clenching his fists like he wasn't done, but the look on his face said that he too had considered his options and knew that it was better to walk away now while it was still his choice to do so.

"We're far from cool," he said, "far from it," he repeated as his eyes darted past Ahmad and straight to me.

"Whatever Q," I said as I started making my way back out of the apartment. Ahmad stopped me, standing in front of me with his arms out and eyes on Q. "Ain't nobody scared of you or your White ass bitch."

"The last I checked, scared didn't mean shit in an ass whipping," Barbie said.

"Oh, she speaks," I said partly impressed by the fact that she had enough balls to step to me and yet angry at the fact that she

48

thought she could. I pushed past Ahmad and got right in her face. "Please don't get it twisted Fatal Attraction, I will floor your dumb ass and not think twice about it."

"Bring it," she said reverting back to the corny state I thought she came from. That made me laugh, she really thought she said something. I laughed so hard I spit in her face and gave no apologies for it.

"I'm too through," I said as I wiped tears of laughter from my eyes, I walked back into Ahmad's apartment with no intention of rejoining this crazy situation. I didn't care what Q or Barbie decided to do, but whatever it was, it was not going to include me.

Ahmad came in minutes after I did. I didn't even bother asking what happened after I left the scene, it really didn't matter.

As much as I...

said it didn't matter it did. My emotions were having a fight with themselves. "So," I began, "it looks like you knew about this all along." A lump formed in my throat at the thought of betrayal. Ahmad, Q, there was no one I could trust. I was honest with both of them, which is the least they could have extended to me. And to be playing me to the left for some White chick was beyond bearable.

"Alyssa, don't come in here and try to turn this shit on me. You knew your life was fucked up before I even entered the picture."

"Wow, why don't you say what you really mean, Ahmad. I mean it's not like I just saw my husband all hugged up with Barbie. Then to find out that they are your neighbors, and oh let's not forget that a man who has never hit me before just smacked the shit out of me. So please, let's not spare my feelings here at all."

"Don't try to play the victim, it doesn't become you. I was there just like you. Let's begin with the fact that you saw that shit because you were here trying to get with me."

Shock must have clearly shown on my face. A poker face I never had.

"Exactly," Ahmad continued, "and as for him smacking your ass, I ain't got no words for that shit, but it didn't look like you was gone need no help with that either."

I crossed my arms and sat back on Ahmad's couch. He was pissing me off. I wasn't trying to play the victim. At least I didn't think so. I just wanted some answers with a little sympathy on the side.

"Whatever, Gary," I said as I put my face in my hands trying to make sense of it all. It was one of the only times I had called him by his first name, but right now I didn't think he deserved the nobility of Ahmad.

Always on point, the name thing didn't get past him. "You know," he started as he headed for the door and put his hand on the knob, "I ain't never been one that had to make a chick stay."

"Don't flatter yourself sweetie," I said as I jumped from the chair and headed to the door, "in my mind, I was already two steps ahead of you."

He opened the door, I exited, never looking back, never feeling the need to.

If I was...

the type who had to depend on another substance to get me through every minute or hour that pained the very core of me, then I would have headed straight to the closest night club and had my fill. Unfortunately, my drinking days were limited, I didn't too much care for it, the best I could do was a wine cooler every six months. There were other rare occasions, but most times it would be when Tee was around me, because undoubtedly she would finish every drink I started, leaving me slightly tipsy and far from drunk.

Therefore, I had to lean on my own dependency. I drove and let the wind hit my face to dry the tears faster than they could fall. Then I would stop randomly, think and write. It was almost midnight when I finally made it home. I was extremely exhausted; otherwise I may still have been out there driving.

To my surprise Q's car was parked in the garage. I sat in the car a moment trying to collect my thoughts. I didn't know what I was about to enter into or how I would handle it. As I drug myself out of the car, I knew that I didn't have the energy to handle any of it tonight. I decided to go up the backstairs to the apartment.

The site that I saw when I opened the door gave me a sudden jolt of energy. Q was lying in the bed with his back turned toward me.

"Oh no the hell you're not!" I said as I slammed the door and stormed toward Q.

"Alyssa, don't come home starting this shit." Q said calmly. He almost made me think that I had dreamed the day's events.

"What the hell? Are you kidding me?"

"No, I'm not," Q said as he sat up in the bed exposing his well-built chest and hard abs. I was not fazed, today's events left me numb to any excitement from him.

"Okay, so if this is not some type of joke," I said as I walked over to the dresser and laid my keys down, "then why are you in the apartment, let alone the house?"

Q crossed his hands over his chest, reminding me again that he didn't have on a shirt. "It seems you have forgotten the Judge's orders" Q said between clenched teeth mocking the fact that I had gotten us into this situation.

"Q, not tonight, tonight is not the night for this mess. You smacked me and right now it's taking everything in me not to jump on top of you and beat the shit out of you for that."

"And you didn't deserve it?" Q said as he climbed out of the bed and headed toward me.

"You deserve far worse," I said as I clenched my fists preparing for a fight for the second time that day. Before I could move Q had wrapped his arms around me and started squeezing me tight, I wrestled with him to let me go, but I was no match for his strength.

"Stop fighting me, Alyssa. I am not now nor will I ever be your enemy."

"Fine," I said still struggling against his hold. "Just let me go." The touch of his embrace and the smell of his cologne were willing me to forget things I knew that I couldn't. Q slowly released his grip on me staring me in the eyes as if he could read what my next move would be.

Drained from the day's events, I didn't have it in me to fight anymore. I turned away from Q and went to take a shower. I let the water run over every part of my being, praying that when it was done, I would feel better.

The shower door opened and instinct made me cover myself with my hands. "Q, now I know you're tripping," I said as I watched him walk into the stall naked.

"Come on, Alyssa, after eight years of marriage, I doubt very seriously you have anything to hide that I haven't seen a million times."

"That may be the case, but right now, I have everything to hide. You don't own the same privilege anymore, Q."

"I wouldn't speak those words so quickly if I were you," he said as he closed the shower door forcing our bodies to touch. I tried to make my way around him.

"Look, you can have the shower, I was done anyhow," I said as I made a failed attempt to open the shower door. Q grabbed my hand softly and placed it on his waist.

"Alyssa," he started, "seeing you with ol' boy today did something to me. I can't explain it, but all I know is for the first time in a long time, I knew I didn't want to lose you." He kissed me lightly on the forehead.

I lifted my head and allowed anger to fill my eyes. "So that's what this is about, your jealousy. Suddenly you want me, after almost two years of me trying to force you to see me. Are you serious, Q?"

"It's not jealousy, it's want, it's love. I want you not because another man does, but because I do. You're the only woman that could ever make me feel jealousy; that could make my heart stop beating with just the thought of you being in anyone's arms but mine."

"So like I said," I folded my arms so that our bodies would not be so connected, the water continued to cover both of us as it made its way from hot to warm. "You're jealous."

"Are you listening to my words," Q said as frustration lines etched into his forehead, "this isn't about jealousy, not on its own, it's about love. Do you still love me, Alyssa?" he said as he grabbed my arms.

"Let me go, Q," he dropped my arms and I walked out of the shower. Q didn't stop me this time, I noticed his defeated expression in the mirror but I couldn't let Q get the best of me, I had to keep moving, I couldn't let his words move me in any way. Once I was dressed for bed, for the first time since we moved into this home, I headed downstairs to the guest room. If Q was insistent on having the apartment, there was nothing I could do about it, but I would make darn sure that he wouldn't have me.

THE SMELL OF...

turkey bacon, grits, cheese eggs and cinnamon rolls greeted my nostrils the moment my mind awakened the next morning. I rolled over groggily emotionally weak from yesterday's events. Part of me wanted to stay in bed with the hopes that if I didn't leave it, I would never have to face Q, Ahmad or Tiffany. That would be too easy. I sat up and ran my fingers through my hair, picked up my cell phone to check for missed calls or messages. I placed it back on the night stand and rested my head on the headboard.

The door to the guest room crept open slowly, Q walked in with a breakfast tray. My face went from expressionless to anger in a matter of seconds. I crossed my arms and turned up my lips.

"I'm not hungry," I said before he could fully enter the room. My stomach growled loudly exposing my lie. I moved my hands from my chest to my stomach, praying to muffle the sound but it was in vain as it growled again.

"Uh, I hate to be the bearer of bad news, but sounds to me that either your mouth or your mind needs to have a meeting with your stomach before they draw that conclusion," Q said as he laughed at my lie. "Besides, I put my foot into this meal, so why deny yourself a taste of heaven."

"Whatever, Q" I said as I made no attempt to reach for the tray that he held out before me. He sat the tray on my lap, everything looked perfect. My mouth began to water. "Can you please get your little breakfast off my lap? Thank you, but no thanks."

"Why are you so stubborn, Alyssa?"

"Hmmm, stubborn, let's see, maybe it's because I caught my husband coming out of an apartment happily in the arms of another woman, a White woman at that. Or maybe, just maybe it has something to do with the fact that my husband put his hands on me in the worst way. Or maybe,"

"Okay, Alyssa, I get it. You have a list of reasons to be angry, and so do I. You are not as innocent as you are making yourself seem. Are we forgetting why you found out about Tiffany or why I slapped you? Let me refresh your memory to the fact that you were heading into an apartment of your own with a half-naked man that I told you the first night he called was inappropriate."

"Were you making a point?"

"Stop sweeping everything under the rug, trying to be passive when you should be aggressive. You don't want me the way that I do you, that's obvious. If you did, you would be fighting for this marriage with me not against me."

I gave him a round of applause before handing the tray back to him. "It's so nice of you to give me the same speech I gave you over a year ago. So what, now that you can confirm that another man want's me, you have developed a desire to work on our marriage and I'm just supposed to forget everything that has transpired that tells me otherwise?"

"First thing, that brotha don't want you, he wants to fuck you, understand the difference. Second, when you step to me with your accusations, step correct. Alyssa, our marriage has been falling apart at the hands of both of us, not just me. It shouldn't matter what triggered the reaction, what is important is the fact that I'm genuine, and that's a lot more than I can say for ol' boy that you feelin' way tougher than he feelin' you and that's real talk."

I wasn't prepared to cash Q's reality check. Ahmad's being fully aware of Q's infidelity had left a bitter taste in my mouth, one that made me never want to deal with him again, so Q didn't have to push any buttons to close that door. It was already sealed tight; however, I refused to believe that I was nothing more than sex for him, so I made a mental note to call Ahmad on it. As for Q, the bridge between us had a fire burning too hot for us to turn back, there was no more us.

I stared at Q. I had no response for him. Sadness filled my eyes, pain filled my heart. I moved the covers from my body, got up and walked past him without another word. There was too much for me to digest right now.

CAN WE TALK...

I asked Ahmad as I sat in my sitting area remembering the last conversation that I had with him in this same position.

"Didn't think you would call my line again?"

He sounded smug and I hated him for it, but I pressed on because I needed answers, my heart had a void a mile long right now. I refused to believe that I had been played, there had to be more to what we had.

"Honestly," I said as I let out a deep breath, "I didn't think I would either. Hurt doesn't begin to describe my feelings right now, but that's not why I'm calling. I just really need to talk to you, and I would prefer to do it in person if you're up to it?"

The silence seemed to last forever although not even a minute had passed before he said, "I'm cool with that, under one condition."

"Oh, so now you have requirements?" I said trying my best not to show my aggravation that was increasing by the minute. Q had voiced an opinion that I was beginning to hear more than I cared for lately.

"Yes, and that's exactly why, Alyssa. Listen to your attitude."

Humph, I thought, I guess I wasn't as discreet with it as I thought. Definitely have some work to do on that poker face. "I'm sorry, Q and I had another falling out; it just has me in a mood. What are your conditions?" Apologizing tightened my face even more. I had to bite my lip before I said something that would leave me without answers completely.

"Leave the drama with Q; I'm not feelin' that today."

I swallowed the lump that formed in my throat, took a sip of water to calm my nerves, before I responded, "So what's your condition?"

"That was it, you can stop by in an hour, but I'm serious Alyssa, if you're coming with a bunch of drama, don't come."

Before I could respond, he hung up. The writing was on the wall. There was no need for me to go, my answer was clear. Somehow having this confirmation in my mind did nothing for confirming it in my heart. So like the fool people believed me to be, I found myself dressed and in the car heading to Ahmad's, if for nothing else but to make matters worse.

Surprisingly, I made it to Ahmad's within the hour he had requested, assuring that I was looking nothing less than gorgeous, because if it was within my control, this would be the last time Ahmad would be so blessed to see my face again, much less my assets.

I looked around the lot and was relieved that neither Q nor Tiffany's car was parked there. I hopped out of the car with my heart racing, nervous at what I was about to find out, but determined to face this head on. If I was as honest with myself as I was with others, I would have to admit that this was just a poor attempt at seeing Ahmad again. As much as I wanted to be over him, I was far from it.

I had only been to Ahmad's place a few times, yet each time that I was here, he always greeted me at the door before I even got out of my car, this time was different, but so was this visit. I knocked and waited patiently for him to respond. When the door swung opened, I half expected him to be in pajama bottoms with no top. Ahmad wore black slacks with a button up shirt to match, and black Stacy Adams. He looked as if he was going to or coming from a business meeting, for whatever reason, it made him look older and surprisingly, more appealing.

He stepped to the side giving me room to enter. I passed him smelling of Chanel No5, purposely adding more sway to my hips as my Donna Karan jeans hugged me lovingly. My 3 inch shoe boots gave me the height that I needed so that his 6'3 wouldn't intimidatingly tower over me.

I turned like a model on the runway and placed my hands in my back pocket. My thighs were plump and looking as if they were begging to be parted, I wore a black V-neck that dipped into my D cups perfectly, exposing the creamy smooth skin. I had just had my hair styled in a silk wrap with my ends colored honey blonde. My hair lay on my shoulders softly, effortlessly. If I knew nothing else, I knew that I could not look any better than I did at that moment.

Ahmad closed the door and then stared at me, not for long, but long enough to cause the erection that was apparent through his slacks, and that was good enough for me.

"Did you come to model or talk?" he asked, breaking the momentary silence we were in.

"So cute," I said not at all impressed, "if you were the gentleman I once thought you were; you would have offered me a seat instead of cutting some smart remark."

"Oh, so I see you coming in the door breaking the condition. Just as quickly as you flew down that highway to see me, you can flip the direction from whence you came. To your husband," he said as he waved his hand in the direction of his front door.

"What happened to you?" I asked as I walked toward him and stood directly in front of him.

"Nothing happened to me, what happened to you?" Ahmad walked past me and sat down on the couch, "oh my bad, did you want something to drink?"

"No, I don't" I said absently as I followed suit and sat in the chair across from him. I positioned myself on the edge and rubbed my hands across my thighs before placing my hands in my lap. My palms weren't sweaty; I think I did it to calm my nerves. Each moment that passed showed me what I was too blind to see before and the revelation was painful.

"So what's up, Alyssa" Ahmad said as he tapped my knee lightly, "what do you want to talk about?"

The way he said the words made me feel childish, I sat straight up to regain my confidence. "You," I said as I stared him in the eye, searching for the degree of honesty that he would give me today.

"Okay," Ahmad pushed back further in his seat and crossed his legs. "What do you want to know?"

"Did you play me?"

"Let me school you real quick baby girl," I had to stop my lip from curling at Ahmad suddenly trying to sound street. "The only person that can play you, is yourself. You decide what you will and will not accept, not me. So the answer to your question is no."

"Okay, I see that you want to go the indirect way. Then answer me this, did you ever love me?"

"Alyssa, I ain't never told you I loved you. I care about you, I always have and I probably always will, but love ain't never entered the picture."

"You know as much as I am appreciating the honesty you want to bring, I hate you for it just the same. I really wish you would have just left me alone."

"I did leave you alone; you kept chasing me until I didn't have the strength to run anymore."

"Chase you? Oh so now I was chasing you, Ahmad? I could have sworn that pendulum swung both ways, but it's all good. I see your vision clearly."

"Alyssa, you want to make a big deal about words. You and I both know that I tried respecting you, your marriage. I had to threaten you with a restraining order, so don't play dumb now. As attractive as I think you are, the truth is, you're not all that. Not to ruin my religion with Allah."

"You know what, I had no idea until now," I said as I stood and walked past Ahmad, when I reached his door I turned back around and said, "I am too good for you and your bullshit."

I walked out the door with my head held high, I had no intention of ever and I meant ever seeing Ahmad again. This was the closure that my heart needed. I will not lie and say that it didn't hurt because it did, it hurt like hell, but I knew my worth and I was not about to let Ahmad make me think less of myself.

I DIDN'T WANT TO...

but my heart was betraying my mind as tears flowed uncontrollably down my face. My thoughts were filled with anger the whole ride home, my face had been so contorted that my jaws hurt. None of that mattered when I got back home to the comfort of the apartment. All the words that Ahmad said hit me like a ton of bricks. I kept replaying the relationship from start to finish, wondering what I had missed. How could I have been so naïve to the truth in his intentions? I paced the floor, the silence was killing me, I wanted to hit him, but I would never let him know how much he hurt me.

I walked over to the nightstand and grabbed my cell phone, clicked on contacts; his name was at the top of the list. I took a deep breath, closed my eyes, and let the memories of what was us replay in my mind, I exhaled, opened my eyes and watched the silent tears make their way from my cheeks to the face of my phone as I pressed delete.

I stormed over to the entertainment center as if it was the one that spewed venomous words my way, slammed the door open and began looking through my collection of CD's. I found one that I had a DJ friend of mine put together for me. It was perfect for this occasion. I went downstairs and grabbed a flute and bottle of red wine. Drinking was becoming a regular habit for me lately, I needed to find another outlet, but I wasn't about to start tonight.

After pressing play, I went to the closet and stripped. Obviously, my attire did not have its intended effect on Ahmad. In its place were Q's pajama pants and a wife beater. I flopped down on the lazy boy recliner with wine in hand as I sipped and let Keri Hilson sing my emotions through song. *Energy* blasted through the player as my heart felt the pain of each word.

She was the first artist but not the only one who would rip my heart into shreds through the night with songs they used to entertain the world. Dionne Farris' *Hopeless* followed her and that was exactly how I felt right now.

I was mad at myself for being foolish enough to give Ahmad a part of me that I could never get back. I allowed him to open my nose so wide that I betrayed my vows. It didn't matter whether Q was faithful or not, I gave my vows just as he did and until Ahmad, I had remained true to them. "You suck at life!" I screamed in the dark room as I quietly wondered if I meant the words for Ahmad or myself. I was on my third glass when Q walked into the room with Heather Headley's *In My Mind* filling the room.

"Who sucks at life?"

His words startled me, his presence was hit or miss, sometimes he would be there and sometimes he wouldn't, my feelings were becoming numb to that fact too.

"I don't know," I answered as Q flicked the light on.

"Damn, you look like death warmed over."

"Nice to see you too," I said as I took another sip of my wine, feeling like a true drunk.

"So you went to see him, didn't you?"

"Who?"

"Come on, Alyssa. We are too grown for silly games; you know I'm talking about Gary."

Q still refused to call Ahmad by his last name and even after what he put me through, I still refused to call him by his first. Gary made him sound weak. I believe we both understood this when we made our choices.

"Yes, Q, I did." I finished my wine then set the empty glass on the floor next to me.

"I guess it didn't go the way you wanted it to either. Are you finding out that he's not really the man that you created him to be in your mind?"

I reached back down for my glass, walked over to the cabinet and grabbed the bottle of wine, poured another glass and took a gulp. I would need this and more to have this conversation with Q.

"It looks like he's every bit of who you made him out to be though," I said as I lifted my glass in salute to Q. "Congratulations."

"Alyssa," Q said as he walked over to me, "I wasn't trying to hurt you. I was trying to inform you. You're so busy trying to cut me down and lift up another man that you didn't want to see him for who he really was. I told you from day one dude wasn't no good."

"Does it really matter what you intended when the result is the same, Q? I'm hurt, disappointed, angry, frustrated, do you have any other emotions you want to send me through right now?"

"Yes, I want you to be happy. I want you to remember what it feels like to love and be loved. I want you to remember us, Alyssa. We weren't all bad."

"What happened to Barbie?"

"Alyssa, her name is Tiffany, and she is not the subject at hand right now."

"I know it is but Barbie just fits her so much better, don't you think?" I asked rhetorically as I took another sip of my wine. I was starting to feel a little tipsy. I was glad, my thoughts were no longer on how Ahmad played me. I was just enjoying being me. I started swaying to the beat of a Jill Scott song and throwing my hands in the air like I really was on a dance floor in a club.

"How much have you drank?"

"Have some?" I said as I lifted my glass to Q. Q reached for my glass but he did not drink, he placed it on top of the cabinet.

"No, Lyssa, I don't want any and it seems like at this point, you shouldn't want any either. You really love him don't you?"

Q's question came just as K'Jon's *I'll Never Forget* hit our speakers, my mind and heart couldn't take the combination. My knees felt weak, I grabbed my stomach and went down, tears fell fast, hard. I didn't care how I looked to Q right now. I cried so hard my body shook. The room went dark, without opening my eyes I knew that Q had just turned the light back out. I was happy that he understood; I needed to be alone right now. I didn't need conversation or light, I just needed to let my soul breathe and for me, this was the best way to do it.

I soon found that I was right in some ways and wrong in others, Q did know what I needed, but it wasn't to be alone. I felt him kneel down to the floor with me he leaned against the wall and pulled me toward him. He let me cry, tears and snot over another man on his shoulder. It was unheard of, and yet it was happening. I let him hold me, comfort me, until my tears dried and the music stopped. We awoke the next morning in this same position, I felt better, with the exception of the pounding in my head and the crick in my neck.

I stretched, which woke Q. He looked at me and said so sincerely, "I love you."

I replied, "I know."

I WASN'T QUITE SURE...

how I felt about Jayla. She had given many impressive comments during our last meeting and for that I had gained respect for her, but for some strange reason, I was still cautious of her. She and Tee were getting closer by the day, going to the mall or the movies. It was always something. Now, Tee had suggested we meet at Jayla's place for hot topics.

Of course I was a little put-off by this because to my knowledge Jayla wasn't actually a part of the hot topics group. I knew that I was being childish, so I took down her address. Apparently she and I didn't live too far apart because I was the first to arrive. Needless to say, Jayla's home was gorgeous. Her upper level, which I did not venture into, was built like a loft overlooking the lower level. Her taste in furniture was to die for.

She had installed marble floors in the kitchen and dining area. Turned the dining area into a relaxation room, changed the living room into a formal dining room with an exquisite set that was made of white Italian leather. Her family room had hard wood flooring and she placed an accent chair beneath her television, which was so uniquely creative, I found myself again gaining more respect for Jayla.

I sat in the kitchen where she had placed an array of hors d'oeuvres. I placed a few of the cheeses on a napkin and began to snack. "So, do you have a subject yet, Jayla?" I asked trying to break the ice and prayerfully place us on better ground.

"Ummm," she said and for the first time I noticed that she had an accent, it was southern but chic, I would have guessed it to be Texan, but I wasn't sure. "I was thinking about talking about that man, who is just that one, you know," she said as she did a little dip for emphasis.

I guess the devil wanted to use me to rear his ugly head because before I could stop the words from exiting my lips they hit the air with attitude that did not get past the radar, "And that's different from our last topic, how?"

"I see you still on that bullshit," Jayla said as she put her hand on her hip.

"I'm not trying to be Jayla, I promise I'm not, it's just something about you that rubs me the wrong way," I said as I placed my napkin of cheese down on the table.

"You don't even know me, so how could I possibly rub you any way?"

"I don't know, I guess it's just the way you say things out the side of your mouth, real slick like. It's like you drop sarcastic remarks and sometimes outright lies and you don't expect anyone to call you on your own bull, and that irritates the mess out of me. Plus, you walk around like you own the world and that gets under my skin too." I was surprisingly calm; it made me realize that this wasn't a confrontation, just a conversation of differences between adults that could be handled like adults.

"Look little girl, I'm not about to apologize for being me, I like me just the way I am, so I'm sorry that I don't fit into some

74

package that you're trying to create, but you need to deal with that on your own terms and leave me the hell out of it."

"Now see this part of you, I like. You don't take anything from anyone, and your confidence is off the chart. Just like you, I like me too and I don't change for anyone but myself. That's not the issue."

"Well, whatever the issue is, I'm not about to make it my problem, it's yours and that's where I'm leaving it." With that said, Jayla and I both decided there was nothing more that needed to be said for that conversation. I picked up my cheese and continued to snack, waiting for everyone else to arrive.

Emauri and Tee came in together. Tee was laughing as she walked through the door like the party came with her.

"What up, Lyss, I see you made it here timely?" she said as we hugged.

"Nothing much," I said then I whispered in her ear, "Let's pray this evening goes better then it started. Your girl is already tripping."

"I heard that shit," Jayla spat looking me dead in the eye as she placed beverages ranging from non-alcoholic teas and lemonades to wines and other alcoholic beverages on a small table that she had set between the kitchen and family room.

"Alright, alright," Tee sang as she went over to the table and made herself a drink, "see now this is what I'm talking about." Tee didn't comment on either of our statements and I know she heard us both.

"So where are Danni and Bree? Are they making their way here today?" I asked Tee and Emauri since I hadn't heard from either of them.

"Now you know I don't know," Emauri said.

"Hell naw," Tee said "Bree doing her family thing right now and Danni got a date with some new dude."

"Humph," I began offended that this would be the second meeting they were missing, "they are M.I.A. quite a bit lately."

"Okay, Jayla," Tee said, "what's up on that topic today?"

"I was trying to tell Alyssa just before y'all came that my topic is a twist on our last topic. So what about the one who is just that brotha! You know that one who you'll just be a fool for! He's that one who brings the best or worst and freak out of you! Doesn't have to be all that fine he just do things that needs to be done and you can't get enough. How many of us have had one of them?" Jayla said as she raised her hand, I felt enlightened on the change of topic. I guess if I had let her say her spiel then I would have noticed the difference between this and the last topic.

"This is the man you marry," I said, "because he has all the right stuff. I wonder though, how many of us lose ourselves in a man like this. Especially someone like me, I find that I am not the same independent woman that I used to be. I have thrown caution to the wind and just leaned into this man, who is all that." Thoughts of Q ran through my mind as I wondered why I was letting Ahmad intrude on my marriage to a wonderful man.

"Ooooooooooo mmmmmeeeeee," Emauri sang. "I have one of those kinds of relationships right now. Do we consider this type a friend with benefits? I actually like it because there is no strings attached it's like I do me and you do you. When I need him he's there and I'm there for him! What kind of relationship do you ladies think it is? Be honest."

"I have to say I'm more with Jayla," Tee said, and I thought, 'no surprise there.' "I wouldn't necessarily marry this person because we all know after a certain time or as years go by the bedroom starts to look a little dim. This man would have to be that

76

'Brotha' the one that makes you so lost for words after everything is said and done. The one that would ask you to do something and without hesitation that shit is done. You don't have to ponder over it you just do it. Every time you close your eyes you're thinking about his last touch and craving and starving for more. The one where you would do it anywhere with so YES! YES!" Tee began shouting and stomping her feet, "Jayla, I did have one of those. Man I'm getting all juiced up thinking about his ass right now."

She took a sip of her drink before she continued, "Emauri, I think that is a friend with benefits relationship, which is also cool, y'all have that understanding that there is nothing between us but friendship and when we are ready to get it in we can get it in, which in my opinion, is the best relationship to have. You can kick it with him and enjoy each other's company without all the extra. There usually is no jealousy or hidden agenda. So I love those relationships too. I have also had one of those."

"Damn! Y'all said exactly what I'm talking about! Tee, girl you hit it when you said 'that shit is done without hesitation'! Whew. I know you know when you said you're gettin' all juiced up. 'That brotha' is the one that you constantly think about because his ass got swag for days and he puts it DOWN," Jayla said as she slapped her hand down hard on the couch.

I thought about her words, their words and wondered if I had ever experienced the man they were all so excitedly referring to.

"That touches on that jealousy issue that Tee mentioned," Jayla continued. "Emauri, girl that benefit thing is a plus especially when he happens to have stature or money so therefore, y'all will do crazy spontaneous shit because money ain't a thang."

Jayla seemed excited that her topic was going over well. She turned her body toward me, pointing her baby finger. "I think he's the one that we don't give a damn about marrying, Alyssa, because both already know the chemistry between the two is SICK and nine times out of ten he's feeling you too. So you already know another bitch can't take care of daddy the way you can."

"Well, I'm no one's dog," I said still not allowing myself to use the harsher curse words. My voice spilled the words a little more prim and proper then I had intended, but they got my point because Jayla immediately jumped in with her explanation.

"I don't consider us as bitches I used that choice of word because that's how we think when we know we got a brotha sprung."

"Jays, please girl," Tee began again shortening Jayla's name in that way too comfortable way, "you don't have to explain yourself. Girl you getting me all fired up."

Jayla almost choked on the cheese she had just popped in her mouth as she stomped her foot and laughed at Tee's comment. "Tee you're a mess! I'm wondering if we as women can really be in a 'no strings attached' relationship as emotional as we are? Now some say we can but I've always said if a woman can just go from man to man without a thought they were just raunchy but maybe I'm wrong."

"Well," Tee said. "I used to think that it was hoe-ish, to jump from man to man, but then I began to say, why can't we have the same freedom as a man. I'm an adult, why can't I enjoy the same kind of pleasures as him. I like different varieties also. It doesn't matter to me what people say about me, as long as I don't start saying the same about myself and feeling bad about it, who gives a damn. I do not let society or anyone else dictate what I do in my life."

"Interesting twist is correct," I said as I looked at each of them, "because what I think I am hearing is that many of you as women are equating yourselves to men." I swallowed hard as I tread lightly, I didn't want to judge anyone for their beliefs; after all we are here to learn, one from the other. "I do not believe that every woman has to marry or there is something wrong with them, but I do believe that there are men that come in your life that you want to marry. For me, the man you have been describing is that ultimate man," I said returning back to my initial thoughts.

"Yet, none of you seem to believe that he is. In fact, you seem more content with keeping the relationship as 'friends with benefits'. I can understand that concept for some points in your life but at what time do you stop being like the average man, stop moving from man to man and marry someone. Another thing I don't believe is that if you do decide on marriage that suddenly your craving for other men will just cease, but if you're marrying that one, then you should be able to keep getting satisfaction from him, regardless to attractions coming and going from other dudes." Ahmad was making himself vivid in my imagination right now, I was mad at myself for allowing my thoughts to so easily sway back and forth between he and Q, it was ridiculous.

"Alyssa, I believe that marrying that ultimate one will not make him the ultimate one as time goes by for this very reason." Tee said, "I think for some reason when you decide to put marriage into the equation it just changes things. Why, I don't know, I have my own reasons but they're not law. I am not a huge fan of marriage because I've been there. I'm not saying that there are not successful marriages, because I'm sure there are. I've not witnessed any personally." This thought made me raise an eyebrow at Tee, I mean she knew everything about me but no one else in the room did, so for her to say this publicly was also admitting that Q and I were having problems.

"I guess I can look at myself as a woman who thinks like a man." Tee continued, unfazed by my disapproving look. "I have been told that on many, many occasions. I just prefer things to stay lit. I'm not saying that the idea of being married is not a good one. I'm wishy-washy when it comes to the subject, but every time I go back and forth with it, I prefer not to be married, maybe as years go on and I get restless and old as hell then maybe marriage will be for me, but until then I will keep my fire and desire."

Tee was sitting strong right now and no one could get an edge in otherwise. She was not through with her words as everyone munched on the snacks that Jayla provided.

"Jayla and Emauri," she said as she looked directly at them and omitted me from her next words, "I know we would love to think that we have no strings attached, but strings start getting in there somewhere, not only for the woman but for the man also, yes we are emotional creatures and sometimes it can be hard for us just to accept that this is just a 'friendship'. I guess as time goes on in the friendship, we will get used to it just being a 'friendship'".

"I think my point is," I began as I placed myself right back in the center of conversation, "that things will change whether marriage is the factor or not, the key is to keep the fire and desire with the change. In the last topic with the poisonous men, you guys hit on longevity as one of the key reasons you stay with the wrong man for so long, so what do you do to stay with the right man? It seems like we as people do not adapt well to change and rather than trying to work out the kinks to that change we would prefer to just move on. I don't agree that there aren't any successful marriages. I think it's how we view successful marriages. To consider it a success if there are no problems is like living in a fairytale land. Any time you are in any relationship of any sort there are going to be problems."

"Well, Alyssa," Emauri said. "I haven't married because I haven't found the right man. It seems that every time I get with someone he turns out to be the wrong one and that pisses me off so I just rather have the friends with benefits relationship! It's difficult to find a good man these days because it seems to me that men our age is set in their ways! Every time I meet somebody new he is married but separated and this is the one who treats me like a Queen. Would I be wrong to continue a relationship with him? I mean seriously, what do y'all think?"

"Alyssa," Tee said, "I thought we were talking about the man that you always have a fire for, not the one where you plan on having a serious relationship with, but the one that turns your world upside down. See with this man you don't see him every day, you see each other when you feel like having every inch of your body turn to mush just from the touch of his hands. Yes, you do determine a successful marriage as to what that individual believes is successful. I am just not one for marriage, so to each its own."

Tee knew the underlying reason for my statement was to undercut her words and validate my marriage with Q. She wasn't the type to squabble over minor things like this and she let it be known in her body language.

"Okay, Emauri" Tee continued after making her point to me clear. "It's really about to get heated now. Me, myself, and I do not believe that it is wrong for you to still see him. I think if he is the one that treats you like all that, then that relationship is between you and that man. I understand completely how you can get involved with someone that either is married or has a woman. I have been in both kinds of relationships. I'd rather not be, but I always find out somewhere in the middle that they are with someone or married. I also believe that everyone comes with baggage, including us. Ours may not be as evident as theirs but we come with it too. I just never really take these types of relationships as serious as that. I take them for what they are and that's sex nothing more and nothing less, it's just sex."

"Okay!" I said as I got up to turn my tea into wine, it was looking like I was going to need something a little stronger tonight. I thought better of it when I got to the table and just poured myself a refill of iced tea. "Y'all are really putting it out there, no holds barred. Well, Emauri," I said as I sat back down with tea in hand, "as unfortunate as the situation is, the truth is the truth. Only you and he can determine whether or not your relationship is wrong or not. I know we spoke before on the topic of whether or not there should be a silent code or pact between women, if we know that he is married or otherwise taken then we back off because fidelity has to begin somewhere. I think it was Danni that said even if one woman backed off, then another woman would step up. So, the question now becomes if this is the man who you feel treats you like a Queen, would you be missing out on the pleasures if you back off, that ultimately he may give to another person."

"And as for your comment, Tee" I said letting her know in no uncertain terms that she should miss me with her innuendo's, but just like her, I was a lady of class and would handle myself as such. "I don't want this to be a question of marriage, because that wasn't what the topic touched on, however, in my opinion you guys were describing that man, that to me, you would want to marry. The marriage topic is another time another place. The fire, and attraction that you're speaking of, I think we have all felt that way to some degree. What I can't stand about that, is having that level of attraction for a man who you will never get to feel his touch nor he yours, for situations just as Emauri described, he's married or worse, you are." I said as my moment with Ahmad replayed in my head and I knew that it would be the first and last time I would ever experience him.

"Alyssa, I've felt his touch and he mines." Tee said smiling widely. "Oh believe that...mmmmmmmmmmmmm. Oh I'm sorry, you were saying?"

"Whatever, Tee," I said pulling her coattails because she and I both knew there was at least one occasion when she couldn't feel the touch of a man she was feeling heavy. "So is that to say you were never feeling a guy tough that you couldn't touch?" I asked wondering if she would allow her lips to form a lie to save face. Normally, Tee carried the same degree of honesty as I did.

"Yeah I was but it was a one sided thang. You know I was feeling him that way, don't know if the feelings were mutual though."

"I'm with, Tee" Jayla said as if some surprise was to come from this statement. They really were two peas in a pod, and I continued to wonder how I wasn't privy of their relationship before now. "It's like I said earlier that this is the guy that you don't marry. Tee makes a great point once you do things get all messed up. As a matter of fact, you don't give a damn about a freaking title because it is what it is. Also, like Tee said, you don't see him every day, but boy oh boy when you do. Actually, that's how you keep it fresh. Now, going back to that emotional thing, we as women almost always get attached especially when he's treating us right, but what pisses me off is when he acts like it's just sex when they are attached as well.

I don't get that whole thing. If he's hitting it right, respects you, and always gives you things, texts or calls with sweet nothings, actually goes out of his way to plan things for you, how are we supposed to feel? So sometimes that sends mixed emotions. I hear you Tee, when you say you don't care about what people say or think because people mess me up as if women aren't supposed to admit that we enjoy sex, that's some bullshit. Note this though; if we do take that route I think that we are to keep our business about it to a select few. I also think that most of us have morals even though sometimes situations can cause us to do immoral things, which is why I don't judge when I hear about a woman cheating on her man because nine times out of ten, she's told him over and over he's not taking care of business in some kind of way, be it sex, finances, he's boring. Black women will verbalize how we feel before we dip. Men have done us wrong since the beginning of time and now women aren't taking it anymore but we handle it different. We can go and have our fun outside and come home as if nothing is going on, unlike men, who lose their minds when they have something new."

I shifted slightly in my seat. As relieved as I was to hear Jayla justify things for me, I didn't want anyone to catch on to the fact that this had become my situation.

"So then this becomes the line of division to how men and women handle relationships of this nature." I said, "I almost felt like you guys were beginning to sound just like men, except you are emotional. I truly believe men do disassociate themselves from situations so they can go without emotions."

"That's true, Alyssa," Jayla said, "but more and more women are beginning to act like men. One reason is because we're more educated than back in the day and because men not being responsible, more women have to handle households, kids and holding down a 9 to 5. Therefore, even though most would love to have the 'perfect man' with the white picket fence home' of a life, they're beginning to take a piece of a man for self-satisfaction."

"I think that everyone gets emotionally attached," Tee said. "Men and women. As much as that man tries to withdraw himself from that woman emotionally the harder it becomes for him to have just a sexual relationship with her. It's something about when a man starts fighting his feelings the more intense the sex is. Yeah, Jayla, I do believe that's where I am today, I just want a piece of a man. I don't need the American dream. To your point, Alyssa, I try my best to keep a 'man's attitude' because I don't want to become emotionally attached either."

"I agree with the fact that we do take a piece of a man for satisfaction," Emauri chimed in, "well I did because I have been hurt so many times and being verbally abused to the point that I started to believe that I was worthless and that no man would want me, but for sex so every time a man shows me some attention I fall right in until one day I woke up and realized that I'm worth more than just a piece of ass. So as far as the American Dream I don't want that either. I tend to find myself acting just like the men do in the relationship."

"I really love our conversations," I said, "I honestly walk away from each topic feeling a little more enlightened to the mindset of today's woman and I thank y'all for that, sincerely."

Everybody nodded their head in agreement, as we wrapped the conversation up and headed to our homes with food for thought on our mind.

ENOUGH WAS ENOUGH...

I had been back and forth between Q and Ahmad trying to find out what the hell was going on. I was never one to make visits to the doctors but my body just wasn't cooperating with me. While I was there I did what seemed natural, confident that I would receive a clean bill of health, I asked to be checked for HIV/AIDS and every other STD.

I smiled as the doctor came back into the office with my results in her hand. I couldn't understand why she couldn't just tell me on the phone, but she insisted that I meet her here.

"Alyssa," she said with her head tilted to the side and the 'I'm sorry' smile plastered on her face. I read the expression clearly, although I didn't know what she could possibly be sorry for.

"Dr. Armstrong," I said as I let my expression mimic hers.

"Seems we have a bit of bad news today, but it really is nothing to worry about."

"Humph", I said as I thought before I spoke, trying to be careful not to offend her. "How can bad news not be anything to worry about?"

I left the office angry. I got in my car driving aimlessly to nowhere in particular and wound up at home. Just as I was picking up the cell to dial Ahmad, the house phone rang. PRIVATE displayed across the screen and a rush came over me, I knew it was Barbie calling, I just hoped she wasn't playing games. I wanted a meeting with her, Ahmad and Q. She was the missing link to this. Between the three of them, somebody had some explaining to do. She and I were the common thread between the two. This circle of destruction made me curse the day I let Ahmad touch me. I pressed talk on the cordless and held the phone to my ear.

"Hello," I heard her voice come through the receiver and my skin crawled at the sound of it.

"Are you talking or you're playing?"

"What do you mean?" she said coyly, but I wasn't buying her innocent game.

"Look, Barbie, you and I both know that you have been playing games on my phone for some time now, what's up?"

"Barbie?"

'Damn,' I thought to myself, how had I let that slip? I had been calling her Barbie for so long I think I really began to believe it was her name. "I may not remember your name, but I know who you are," I said as I tried hard to remember what Q said her name was. My memory wasn't the best, and she had no purpose in my life to give her name a space there anyhow.

"I'm sure you do, but for the record, my name is Tiffany just like the store, oh but wait you're not on that level are you?"

"How 'bout this, how 'bout you come up to my level and stop playing childish ass games. What are you calling my house for?"

"I thought it was time for us to sit and chat, like ladies, none of that fighting nonsense, k?"

"I'm game for meeting, but I want to kill two birds with one stone, literally, but we'll make it metaphorically. Set the meeting with Ahmad and Q as well, let me know time and place."

"My, my, my, aren't we demanding?"

"You called me remember," there was no need to inform her that this meeting was already in progress in my mind before her call. I'll let her believe the ball is in her court, for now.

"I did, didn't I? Okay, I'll get things moving and I'll call you back with the details."

I did like Tee, I hung up. The conversation was over; there was no need for formalities.

TRUE TO HER WORD...

Tiffany called with the details. Surprisingly, everyone had agreed to meet at my place. I could care less, everyone had already been here before, so why make this time any different. After our last little fiasco, though, I refused to come unprepared. If Q dared to lay a hand on me he would be walking with one less toe. It wasn't serious enough to end his life, but it would be a point of fact that if you mess with me, you will get it back two-fold. I placed my Beretta in the small of my back and pulled my off the shoulder baby doll shirt down. I double checked myself in the mirror. I had to make sure that everything was as on point as it could be. I mean, these men had both of us and I was not about to look like the underdog. She can be my equivalent but never my superior.

I heard the garage come up and quickly exited the bathroom, I knew Q was coming home, but I wasn't sure if he was bringing Barbie with him or if she was riding on her own. I bit my lip, "Tiffany," I said to myself, "I have to remember her name is Tiffany!"

I heard Q make his way into the house and decided to make my way down there, before he made his way up to the room. I went down the back stairs and our eyes met just as he was closing the door.

"Alyssa," he said curtly as if we weren't married, as if the last eight years of our life meant nothing. A slight pain inched in my heart at the sound; I willed it away and put on my armor.

"Quan," I returned in the same icy tone he had given me.

"So, why are we meeting?"

"And why would I know the answer to that question, Quan," I refused to call him Q, refused to let this be about the comfort we once shared. I also refused to play my hand. I had my own reasons for this meeting, but this meeting wasn't called by me, it was called by Tiffany, so my answer was truth to a certain degree.

"Cut the bull, Lyssa," he said anger rising with every word. "I know you better than you think I do. You don't agree to meetings without some ulterior motive. So what gives?"

There was no need for me to answer as we both turned our heads to the front door at the sound of the doorbell. My heart began to race, I wasn't sure if it was the fact that I would be seeing Ahmad, or I was becoming nervous about how things were really about to play out. My gut was telling me that this meeting was not going to go as smoothly as I planned. I watched Q walk toward the front door. I touched the small of my back as an added measure. It was there, I knew it was, and I was glad.

I followed Q and stood in the hallway as he opened the door. My heart dropped as Tiffany and Ahmad both greeted him. I wondered if they had driven together. I tried to look past them to see the vehicles, but they were blocking my view.

Quan's expression formed into that of a pit bull as he aggressively pushed his weight in front of Ahmad. I looked at Tiffany as she made her way into our home.

"What the hell do you want?" Q said between clenched teeth.

Ahmad threw his hands in the air defensively. "I don't want to be here no more than you want me to be, my man. Tiff told me it was pertinent that I attend, so if you wanna check somebody, you might want to start with your girl and raise up out my face."

"Q, honey," Tiffany began as she ran her finger down the length of Q's arm then placed her hand into his. "I'm not used to seeing you be so uncouth, what's the matter?"

"Why did you invite him here to my home, Tiffany? Do you have any respect for me?"

"Of course I do, but I thought that you stopped considering this your home ages ago."

I watched as the lovers spat and realized that this could go on forever if I didn't take some control over this quickly. I walked past Q and invited Ahmad in. I could feel the heat of Q's breath against my neck as well as the tension letting me know he wanted to throw me out the door with Ahmad.

Tiffany's eyes roamed our home which made my blood boil. I began to direct everyone toward the office, "Shall we," I said as I lifted my hand and motioned in that direction.

"Why not the living area," Q asked.

"Because," I hissed, "this is not a meeting of comfort," I put my tone in check and calmed back down. I walked to the desk and sat down. It was a clear indication that I was in charge, regardless to who called the meeting. Q sat across from me in one of the elegant white Queen Elizabeth chairs we had. Ahmad sat at the table near the window, closest to the door. I assumed that was in the event that he needed to make a quick get-away. I waited to see where Tiffany would sit. There was an empty seat next to both men. She sat next to Ahmad. My heart skipped a beat, but I think it would have done the same if she had sat next to Quan. I loved both men, how I didn't know. Why it mattered at this point, I wasn't sure. The only thing I can say is that the heart does not heal as fast as you want it to, and when you love a man hard, it definitely needs some time to recuperate.

"So," Tiffany began and I cut my eye at her sharply. I felt as if I had enough hate in my heart for her that I could will her to be dead and she would die on the spot. "I had hoped this meeting could have taken place without the men, I felt that it was time for Alyssa and I to have a woman to woman chat about our little circumstance, but she thought otherwise."

"Okay, Mrs. It. I'm really gone need you to cut through the bullshit," I had turned into Tee. The look that Quan gave me at the sound of my voice spitting curses had not missed me.

"I'm sorry. I prefer that we have a conversation as ladies, presuming that you can behave that way for a brief moment."

I balled my fists, this heifer was really trying me and I was really trying to keep my cool. I thought for a moment and realized, this is where she was trying to take me, she was trying to make me look like a crazy fool in front of two men whose opinion, I valued highly. I got this, I said to myself.

"You know what, you're right," I began, "this whole situation has me uncharacteristically stepping out of my norm, but please enlighten us to why you wanted to meet with me, so that I can return the favor."

"As I am sure it is obvious by now," Tiffany began, "Q and I have been engaged for a year and have been living together for just as long. I was rather upset that you decided to cause a scene at our place of residence. Throwing up fists"

94

I laughed at the sound of her prim and proper voice trying to use terminology that was completely foreign to her. Her little announcement about her and Q caused a sharp pain to cut deep within my heart, however, it was something that I had already suspected so for once in my life; I perfected the poker face, refusing to give her the satisfaction. I could see the disappointed look on her face that it didn't garner the result she was expecting.

"You would laugh," she continued as she tried to cut me a look that really went right past me, it was sad that she was clearly unaware as to how little she meant to my world. "You are as ghetto as they come."

"If that's what you want to believe," I said in a tone that let her know in no uncertain terms how her opinion mattered to me not.

"Listen," Quan finally spoke, I was wondering how long the men would let this silly cat fight go on. "Tiffany, you are better than this," that statement caused a huge lump to form in my throat.

'Oh so she's better than this, but it's right up my alley, huh.' I thought the words that I fought hard from slipping from my tongue.

"You're right, baby. I'm sorry," Tiffany said. The word baby fell off her lips so smoothly and casually that the hairs on my neck stood straight up, my fists started clenching, I looked at Q with hate at the forefront of my mind. I turned and looked at Ahmad, hoping that would ease the tension that was building, it did nothing for me. I was just as over him as I was Q and this whole situation. If I did not have a purpose that was so immediate, so urgent, I would have gotten up from my seat at that moment, walked out the door and never allowed either one of them to cross my path again.

I glanced around the room again, waiting to see who would speak next, when no one showed any signs of having anything to say, I took that as my time.

"Okay, now that the lovebirds have had their piece, I want to know which one of y'all motherfuckers exposed my ass to herpes." I had meant to say it more eloquently. I wanted to bring it across with class, but the anger that was steadily rising told me there was no time for being prissy. The moment I heard Dr. Armstrong tell me that I was exposed to something that I can never get rid of, no matter what medicines I take or don't take, I have had fire burning in my bones and a strong desire to make the person responsible feel every bit of that fire.

Inside this room were the only people who could have exposed me. I listened to Dr. Armstrong tell me that this could have been dormant for years before rearing its ugly head, but I wasn't buying that line even as she threw it. No, everything was telling me that this is a recent occurrence that landed in the lap of one of the three.

Q was the first to remove the look of shock from his face and replace it with anger as he jumped up out of his seat, "You slept with him?"

Humph, I bit my lip. That was a detail that I had not given him knowledge of yet. I forgot about that. Just as remorse was creeping its way into my heart, I was reminded of the fact that he too was having an affair.

"What difference does any of that make," Tiffany responded before I had the chance to, visually upset that Q cared so much. "You're my man; you haven't been with her for years."

"You are right again, Tiffany," I said with a sly smile as I dropped the bomb in Q's lap. "He should be more concerned with the fact that you slept with Ahmad."

Pit bull reared his head once more; if it was humanly possible, smoke would be coming from Q's nostril as he started pacing the floor.

"Somebody needs to start talking a little faster, because right now, I'm not so sure what my next move is going to be." Q spat.

"Okay look," Ahmad said quietly as he looked past my eyes into my soul. It was as if he was hurting with the same pain that filled me. "Alyssa, I will be honest and say that my wife has been diagnosed with herpes as well. I was just as angry as you are right now, but when I spoke to the doctor, he told me that there is no way for us to know its origin. I had to accept that. I have been tested and I am still clean, but you and I both know that I strapped up when we were together."

Q was still pacing back and forth, anger controlling his every move. I watched as Tiffany followed him with her eyes, concern telling her story before she opened her mouth and said, "Q, baby."

I cringed again, I wasn't sure if I would ever get used to another woman calling my husband baby.

"Maybe we should talk alone. We don't need our business in the street like this. Like you said, I'm better than this, we're better than this." Tiffany got up from her seat and walked over to Q, everything she was not saying led me to believe I was on point. She was my origin. She is where it all began, although with Ahmad's confession, I could not negate the fact that he was still a possibility. He wasn't strapped when my lips were wrapped around his manhood, exposing me to whatever he may have.

My mind reverted back to that night and the fact that he refused to allow me a full view of him. That triggered an intense explosion.

"You bastard," I yelled as I slammed my hand on the office desk and stared at Ahmad. Tiffany and Q stared on at the scene like they were watching a movie. Tiffany let an obvious sigh of relief cross her face, which again confirmed for me my thoughts. Although I would never be able to prove anything, neither will I be able to determine what degree of guilt was hers, I knew one thing for sure, she was a far cry from innocent.

"Alyssa," Ahmad stood preparing himself for whatever I might come at him with, he placed his hands out in front of him defensively, "I don't know what you're thinking, but I'm telling you this has nothing to do with me."

"It has everything to do with you. Let's start with the fact that you refused to undress for me, I never saw you completely nude. Were you having an outbreak that night?"

Ahmad looked as if he was defeated but he refused to give in without a fight, "Alyssa."

"Don't keep calling my name, give me the answers that I need to hear," I said as I stood from my seat. "Understand this, you don't owe me any explanations, but you don't owe me any lies either. The truth; however, is another story." I said as my voice become softer, calmer. "You have it don't you?"

"No," he said and everything in his answer told me he had just lied to me. A tear escaped my eye as I again found myself reevaluating the basis of this relationship. I sat down in defeat; there would be no answers here today. The answers would not change the fact that my blood was showing that I was exposed, which meant that I was now carrying the virus.

Surprisingly, Q came over and tried to offer comfort. He slowly pulled me from my seat and into a sweet embrace. My body needed to feel love at that moment, so I allowed my head to fall gently on his chest, forgetting where we were, what was transpiring and whose presence we were in. At that moment we were man and wife again. There is a reason they are called moments, they leave as quickly as they come.

Q was snatched from my arms with such force that I thought it was Ahmad pulling him. My breath caught as I looked into the hateful eyes of Tiffany. My heart betrayed me and reached out to her, as I saw the tears streaming down her face. That didn't last long either.

"What the hell is wrong with you, Q?" Tiffany screamed, and for the first time, I noticed the engagement ring on her finger. I took a quick glance at mine and noticed that it paled in comparison.

"My thoughts exactly," I said in a soft tone barely audible to anyone else in the room. I toyed with my wedding ring and then looked Q in the eye.

"So you're in love?" I asked him as tears forced their way to my eyelids.

"Yes," Tiffany spoke.

My eyes darted toward hers, hate filling every word as I chopped them out slowly, "This is not your conversation!"

"Oh, but it is," she said smoothly and confidently as if I was the one intruding. "As you can see," she said waving the ring in my face as if I couldn't see it otherwise, "we're planning to be married this time next year. Everyone loves him, my friends, parents. Things are just perfect, aren't they baby?" Tiffany began rambling as if I was a friend of hers that she was sharing good news with.

Before my thoughts could process my actions, I had went for my Beretta and was walking slowly toward Tiffany aiming directly for her heart, "I said, this is not your conversation."

"Alyssa," Ahmad's voice cut through the air reminding me that he was still there.

"It's not your conversation either, Ahmad." I said as I didn't even turn his way.

Tiffany showed no fear as I kept my barrel aimed in her direction. I think her balls were bigger than some men. I was impressed that she chose not to cower, especially when it was obvious that I could end her life at any moment.

I watched Q watching Ahmad, his eyes intent as if he was ready to make his move; that let me know that Ahmad was trying to catch me off guard. I couldn't turn toward him because then I would leave myself open for Tiffany, I had to think fast. I had to stay in control. I placed the gun on the office desk and quickly lunged toward Tiffany. I never intended to end her life, but this heifer had made me beyond mad and for that I wanted her to feel physically half of the pain that I was feeling emotionally.

Detroit stood front and center as my fist collided with her jaw, that victory faded as she returned the favor and my jaw felt the weight of her punch. The headlock had never failed me so I went for it. I grabbed her neck tight and pulled her to the floor. She snatched a handful of my hair, as she tried to make her way free from my grip. I did the same with hers, pulling her to the ground with the force of it. She landed face up allowing me the opportunity to jump on her straddle style and land a few punches, she placed her hands in front of her face trying to block my blows. A couple landed on her wrist, the pain of my knuckles landing on bone, halted me for a moment.

That was a mistake; all that did was give Tiffany enough time to wrap her hands around my neck tightly. Her grip was causing me to lose air quickly. I pressed my knee into her abdomen as I grabbed her wrists trying to free myself. Q came up behind me and wrenched me from her grip. I wondered who he was trying to save as Tiffany got to her feet looking as if she was about to lunge for me. I looked for my Beretta on the desk where I had placed it but it was gone, I searched Q and Ahmad's face for a hint of its location. Just as I thought, Tiffany was not done.

She came at me forcefully and landed a punch to the pit of my stomach, Q was still holding my arms in a grip that would not release me. I reared back with my foot as hard as I could and landed my foot directly on his crotch, he released me. I pushed Tiffany hard into the office desk. I felt the hard blow of Q's fist in my back causing me to fall forward in the same place that I just put Tiffany.

Before either of us could regain our balance, Ahmad had pulled his weapon. Q had done the same, letting me know where my Beretta had found a home. It was a face-off and I immediately regretted allowing my emotions to get us in this fatal position. I was nearly 40 years old and I was fighting like a teenager on the street. I was embarrassed. I looked at Tiffany hoping that she could read the apology in my expression.

The front door swung open, I heard Carnell yell, "Yo Ahmad, what are you doing?" My heart jumped, as I prayed that Carnell would not walk into the line of anyone's fire.

"Carnell," I screamed as he made his way toward Ahmad.

Tiffany seized the moment and lunged at me, Ahmad turned toward Carnell, apparently surprised at his entrance. Everyone was moving, everything was happening so fast, until somebody's gun fired. I wasn't sure if it was Q's or Ahmad's. Someone screamed, glass shattered, mayhem had just erupted.

As Grace Would...

have it, Q had sent Ahmad to the hospital with a gun-shot wound to his hand. The bullet went through and through tearing a huge hole in his hand. Ahmad grunted and complained but not once did he cry. I was impressed, my heart wanted to go out to him, but my mind was still upset with the events that had taken place. Apparently, Q did not want to see anyone die that night either, especially not in our home.

Although Tiffany drove Ahmad to the hospital, the police did not forego coming to our front door, questioning Q and I about what went on. I guess that's the plus and minus of living in a neighborhood with people who care.

After leaving us, they headed to the hospital to question Tiffany and Ahmad. I prayed the whole time. I knew it wasn't an accident, but it was what was necessary. Ahmad would have to admit to having a gun as well and also reveal what his intents were for having it.

My prayers were answered a few hours later when we got the call saying that no one was pressing charges. This day had been more hectic than I imagined when I rose from my bed this morning. I went into the apartment to give Q the good news and found him packing.

I didn't try to stop him; in fact, I was relieved that he was leaving. Too much was left unexplained. In all the effort that was put forth for me to get answers, I walked away with none. No one in the room wanted to admit that they were the origin of such ugliness.

I wondered how many times this scenario played out throughout the world and in how many different formats. We were living in careless times. It seemed that no one cared about their health any more, let alone someone else's. The fact that guns were drawn while we were meeting to discuss a disease that had been spread amongst us opened my eyes to the fact that we were creating sexual suicide in more ways than one.

That thought was making the pain that I felt of losing the two men that I loved much easier to bear. It didn't stop the tears from falling, but I needed that relief. My heart hurt, not only for myself, but for everyone in that room that day.

I could see that Tiffany wasn't the monster that I created her to be. Her actions were done out of her own pain. She loved Q just as I did, maybe not as much or not as hard, but she loved him and for that I understood her. It didn't explain her playing the games that she did. I wish that women would stop using useless tactics like the ones that she used as outlets. Right now, I couldn't make that my worry. I had too many more important things in line ahead of it.

THE ROOM WAS...

dark and quiet, neither of them said a word. Tiffany's eyes were swollen and her face was flush from the tears she had already shed. He wanted to hold her in his arms until her pain subsided, but he couldn't afford to add confusion to an already chaotic situation. If he could take his words back he would, but his heart refused to let him. He had never stopped loving Alyssa and it wouldn't be fair to start a marriage with Tiffany knowing this. He knew this the day that he proposed, but Alyssa's constant disrespect for their marriage vows caused him to move full speed ahead caring about nothing but his own happiness.

His heart ached at the pain that was a constant from women who refused to be faithful. Now knowing Tiffany's indiscretions too, he wanted to just live a life of celibacy. It was either that or use women the way they have used him, but he knew his grandmother Beck Mo, would turn over in her grave twice if she knew that he was disrespecting women in that manner.

His life wasn't perfect neither were his ways, but he tried with every breath that was in him, to love the woman he was with, and treat her like the Queen she is. Yet the more he tried, the more he felt his heart being stomped on.

His relationship with Tiffany was a direct result of Alyssa's under appreciation of him. She flaunted Ahmad in his face constantly, with no care for his feelings, insisting he was to blame for not appreciating her.

"Don't I make you happy?" Tiffany pleaded breaking the silence.

"It's not just about happiness, Tiffany."

"Then what is it about, Quan? What am I missing? I've seen her, she's beautiful, but she can't offer you what I can. She's ghetto and you need a lady."

"That's just it, Tiffany. She's not. She is classy, she's beautiful, she's wonderful. This past year we have both been through so much, so yes you've seen her behave in a way that I have rarely seen in the eight years that I have known her. This doesn't make her ghetto, baby. It makes her human."

"Why are you defending her?"

"I would do no less for you."

"We're not the same."

"But my respect for you is."

"She's sleeping with another man, Quan."

"You mean the same man that you slept with, Tiffany? I'm not trying to go tit for tat with you here. This is not what this is about. It's about me. I may not be able to articulate my words the way you guys do, but I know what I want and right now it's not us. This relationship has met its peak baby and it's time for us to move on. I couldn't make you happy now if I tried my hardest, but the way I feel at this moment, I don't want to even try."

He watched as Tiffany's face turned red with anger. He pulled her close to him, no longer caring about the confusion it may cause.

"Tiffany, you're taking this way too personal, baby. Listen and believe me when I say this has nothing to do with you. You are a beautiful woman and any other time in my life I would be

106

overjoyed to have you as my wife. Come on, Tiffany. You and I both know this was not the time for us to start a relationship, much less a marriage. I'm still married."

"A fact that was kept from me, Q. I didn't know until it was too late."

"It's never too late. You know now, you've known for a year, it's never too late."

"Don't give me this bullshit, Q" Tiffany yelled as she pulled herself from his embrace. "You know damned well that I had no idea you were married until a year into our relationship. I had fallen so deep in love with you by then."

"I'm sorry," he said quietly.

"Sorry doesn't begin to cut it. You have turned my life upside down and now you just walk away and I'm supposed to be okay with that."

"This thing has just spiraled out of control, Tiffany. I didn't, don't know where it's going. I'm trying to make it right."

"It's too late for making it right, Q. You can make it better, but you'll never be able to make it right again. I don't know why I'm even giving you these, you don't deserve them," Tiffany said as she wiped the tears from her face. "I guess I'll raise our baby by myself," she said as she placed her hand on her stomach.

"Tiffany, if you are pregnant, you and I both know the baby is not mine."

"Are you accusing me of sleeping around?"

"I'm not accusing you of anything, but you are. Tiffany, we've been living together, but we have never slept together."

"Oh my God," Tiffany said as she flopped down in the chair. The look of embarrassment on her face told him she was reaching for straws with none to hold on to.

"Tiffany," he said as he walked over to her. He needed to find a way to comfort her. The lies that she was now spewing revealed how painful this was for her.

"Save it, you've said more than enough." She placed the key to his place on the table, picked up the bag that she had packed earlier and headed out of the apartment that they had shared for over a year.

He shook his head, disappointed at the turn of events. He never expected Tiffany to lie to him. He knew that she would be hurt by the unexpected break in their relationship, but he just didn't know it would come to this. He refused to sleep with Tiffany until he dissolved his marriage with Alyssa. His ultimate goal was not to cross that line until marriage. He was trying to do things differently because no matter what road he seemed to take, he always found himself at the same destination: in a relationship with a woman who was unfaithful.

It was a cycle that began with his high-school sweetheart Tonya, to his first wife Monica, Alyssa and now Tiffany. Q really was starting to have a heart to heart with his maker. Something had to change, but what he understood that most did not, is that change had to begin with him.

HE WALKED INTO...

the clinic and gave the receptionist a bogus name. He didn't want it in his file just in case Alyssa's accusations proved true. The last thing he wanted was for people to be looking at him as if he had a disease of any sort, and once it became a part of his medical record, it would become a part of him.

"Fill this out and have a seat," the receptionist said as she sat behind the glass window staring at him through wiry glasses with a look of disdain. It was the free clinic, so he assumed she believed herself to be above everyone that came through those doors.

"Do you have a pen?" he asked her as he returned the look of disgust she gave him.

"It's on the clipboard," she pointed and he instantly began to hate the nasal sound in her voice. He didn't bother to say thank you. He just walked away feeling she wasn't worthy of his words or his appreciation.

It took him longer to fill out the short application than it would have normally since he was falsifying majority of the information they were asking for. He took the form back up to the snotty receptionist and had to force himself not to shove it in her face. She glanced quickly over his information.

"You don't have any insurance, Mr. Thomas?"

"This is the free clinic, isn't it?"

"That wasn't the question."

"No, I don't" he lied.

"Have a seat; the nurse will call you back shortly."

He sat down and thumbed through the magazines. They weren't taking his mind off why he was there so he tossed it back down on the table and got up and walked around. He walked over to the vending machine that was in the corner of the waiting room. He browsed the items before deciding that he didn't want anything. He wasn't much of a junk food eater anyway. It was just a way to pass time.

"Last call for Mr. Anthony Thomas," he heard the nurse say while looking directly in his direction.

"Here, I'm right here," he said as he made his way over to the nurse. "I didn't hear you. I must have been in a daze."

"Ummm, humph," she said as she twisted her lips.

"Seriously."

"Look, you ain't got nothing to prove to me, but it wouldn't be the first time somebody came up in here under an assumed name."

He started to argue with the nurse but thought better of it; especially since what she saying was the truth.

"Room 3, Mr. Thomas, the doctor will be in shortly," she said as she placed his chart in the door and walked away.

"Great, more waiting," he mumbled to himself.

"Excuse me," he heard a female voice say as he turned around and faced a short and stout redhead.

"Oh, I didn't see you standing there."

"I'm sure," she said as she grabbed the chart the nurse had just placed in the door. "Now, what are you in here for," she asked as she followed him into the examination room.

"No disrespect to your qualifications, but for personal reasons, I would like a male doctor, please."

"You can like what you want, but unless you are paying for this with your insurance, you get what we have. Now again, how can I help you?"

He felt uncomfortable speaking about his issues with a lady. He put his reservations to the side and pressed on. He was glad that he wasn't attracted to the lady, which would have made the situation harder to handle.

"I would like to be tested for STD's."

"Okay, are you currently experiencing any symptoms?"

"No," he thought for a moment, "no, I'm not."

"Mr. Thomas, if you want us to help you, you have to be honest."

He went on to tell her the reasons why he was there. After a half an hour examination that included being poked and prodded he was told he could come back for his results in 3 days. He hated having to wait so long to get results, he didn't want his life held up any more than it already had been, but he didn't have much choice in the matter.

I Opened the...

door to two dozen long-stemmed red roses in full bloom. A smile escaped my face as I remembered a time when Q would send these to my job every week as a reminder of how much he loved me. It had been years since he'd done it.

I reached into my pocket and pulled out a five-dollar bill. 'Oh well, it would have to do' I thought as I extended it to the delivery man.

"No thank you," he said "it's been taken care of."

"Oh," I said as I slipped the five back into my pocket.

I pulled the card from the flowers and read the sweet gesture.

If there is anyone more beautiful than you, I have yet to meet them. My heart is in your hands.

He didn't sign it, but he didn't need to. I placed the roses on the foyer table and admired their beauty as the doorbell rang again. 'I must be really popular today,' I thought. I opened the door to find Q standing on the other side. I smiled, before I remembered all that our marriage was sustaining right now. My smile quickly left.

"Don't be like that, Lyss."

"Where's your key?"

"I don't have one. My name is Q, we met the other day and I was just wondering if you weren't doing anything, can I take you out tonight?"

"Real cute," I said partially impressed.

"I'm serious," he said as he took my hand into his, which I immediately snatched back. "You know what I think?" He asked unfazed by the attitude I was giving him.

"What is that?" I said as I crossed my arms over my chest and twisted my lips in disbelief.

"I think that I can make you love me."

"I never stopped loving you, Q."

"You didn't let me finish, ma'am. I can make you fall in love with me. See, this is something that I have been up all night thinking about. You and I, we're like peanut butter and jelly."

"What?" I laughed amused by his choice of words.

"They're good a part, but so much better together."

"Depends on who you ask," I said not letting my wall down. I wasn't sure where Q was coming from with this newfound 'woo Alyssa' moment, but I wasn't having it and if he was serious about putting our marriage back on track then he would have to do a lot more than send flowers.

"Well, how do you like yours?"

"It depends on the day, I can take it or leave it" letting Q know that I wasn't on the same bandwagon he was. I would have loved to work on our marriage before Ahmad, before Tiffany, before being exposed to herpes. He didn't want to then, so why should I want to now.

"Can we talk?"

"I thought we were."

"Inside, Alyssa."

I stepped aside. Q walked in and stood in the foyer. "Where can we talk?"

"You lead the way."

"Actually, I would prefer if you do. This is your home, not mine and I am respecting it as such."

"Whatever, Q. You can cut the bull, what do you want to talk about."

"I'm serious, Alyssa. I want us to start over. Yes, I will continue making the payments, but I will no longer be living here. In fact that's one of the things I want to talk to you about," he said as he placed the key in the palm of my hand.

"You're serious."

"Dead," he said.

"Okay," I said "you've piqued my interest, why don't we have a seat in the living room."

"After you," Q said as he extended his hand. I led the way to the living room and sat down.

"I'm all ears, Q" I said giving him the floor.

Q sat down next to me, a little too close. I slid over so that he didn't get the wrong impression. I agreed to a conversation, nothing more.

"Okay," Q said as he shifted his body and moved slightly which put more distance between us. "I once read that one of the biggest mistakes a man can make is giving another man an opportunity to make his woman smile. I made that mistake. What I didn't understand then, I understand now. I'm not condoning your actions, but I now see my fault in the situation. I wish that you had come to me sooner and told me what you needed."

"Q," I said cutting him off. "You were doing so well. You were taking responsibility, now here you go pointing fingers and placing blame. I did come to you several times and told you what I needed. The situation with Ahmad didn't unfold without you having a front row seat to the event."

"Okay, I guess I didn't realize how serious the situation was."

"Maybe what you didn't realize is that I would actually leave. You feel that I am so dependent on you and the things that you provide that I would never fathom the idea of leaving you. What you don't understand or realize is that the only person I truly depend on is God. I was independent before you and I can be independent after you."

Q smiled, then clapped his hands together lightly. "Actually, that's one of the things that made me fall in love with you."

I smirked. "Apparently it's one of the things that made you fall out of love with me too."

"I never fell out of love with you, Alyssa."

"Then what's with the apartment on the other side of town, Q? What's with Tiffany?"

"Alyssa, you and I both know that our marriage wouldn't have survived as long as it has, if I hadn't had the apartment."

"News flash, Q, it hasn't."

"Alyssa, I know it's going to be hard for you to put your guard down, but you have to at least try."

"For what, so you can finish what you started and place daggers deeper in my heart."

"I never meant to hurt you, can you say the same thing. What is your relationship with Gary about?"

"First that relationship is over. Second, it wasn't about hurting you. It had everything to do with me. He fed me mentally in a way that I had been begging you for years to do. He listened to me when I talked and spoke in ways that caused me to want more out of life."

"And I didn't? Alyssa we have built a life together. Grant it, it's only been eight years, but look at what we have accomplished."

"You're right Q, we have accomplished a lot together, but sometimes that isn't enough and that's the point that you keep missing. You keep looking at our financial gain and thinking that's all we need to make a marriage work. There's so much more that's needed. Money is only a fraction of what it takes to make life work let alone marriage."

"Then teach me, Alyssa."

"You have to be willing to learn."

"I am."

Q was taking us in the right direction. My heart was warming to him, but I just couldn't give in and I darn sure couldn't trust him.

THE DOORBELL RANG...

and I opened it with a big Kool-Aid smile thinking it was another surprise from Q. I wish I had looked through the blinds because not only was it not a surprise from Q, it was the last person that I wanted to see right now.

"How can I help you?" I said as my lips went from smiling to curling instantly.

"Can I come in?"

"Hell naw," I said as I stepped out and closed the front door, turning the lock to make sure I wouldn't lock myself out. "What do you want?"

"He left me," Tiffany confessed.

"Listen, I don't mean to be rude, but on second thought, yes I do. What does that have to do with me? We aren't girlfriends by a long shot, so why are you bringing your drama to my front door."

"I think he's going to try and work things out with you."

"And that would concern you how?"

"I'm just wondering if you plan to keep him?"

I laughed, a hearty laugh, this heifer had more balls than I had ever given her credit for. "Are you done?"

"Alyssa, I didn't know that he was married. I fell in love with him well before I was privy to that information."

119

"That didn't stop you from playing childish games once you did find out."

"What was I supposed to do?"

"I don't care enough to put thought to what you should have done, but I know one thing's for certain, calling me should have never been on your list of things to do. What were you hoping to gain?"

"I don't know, I guess I felt like if you knew that he was sleeping with someone else then you would leave him, since it was obvious he was moving at a snail's pace leaving you."

"Let me give you a few words to the wise on the off chance you find yourself in this predicament ever again. There is no need to call the other woman or the wife, if you are willing to deal with the situation that man placed you in, then deal with it. That is between you and him. Don't involve another woman in your mess when it comes time for you to clean house. If you're not willing to be the other woman then leave, if he loves you, then that should be enough for him to leave the other woman alone, if he doesn't well, enough said."

"You don't understand, it's more complicated than that."

"No, you don't understand that it's not."

"I'm pregnant."

"Okay, you didn't hear a word, I said. That has nothing to do with me. That is your personal business, so deal with it as such."

"It will have something to do with you, if you stay with Quan. Are you going to help him raise our baby? Do you want to see the product of his affair every weekend? Or how about the child support, how are you going to feel when your finances are affected by our love?"

"The same way I do right now. Please leave my home and don't come back," I said as I turned and walked away from

120

Tiffany's drama hoping that I made my point very clear to her although I could see in her eyes that I hadn't. She was a woman scorned and much more than that, she was a woman who was hopelessly in love with a married man. I knew her pain, because I was that same woman, twice, but it was a woman that I would put every effort into never becoming again.

To say That I ...

was in no mood for company, hot topics, girls night or anything of the such, was an extreme understatement. This past week had been hell on wheels and I would make good company for absolutely no one. However, Emauri had become more regular than Bree and Danni. I couldn't let her down. Tonight we were meeting at her house, so I made this the priority in my mind.

Emauri did not live in the best of neighborhoods and she did not have the best of homes either, however, she made it her home and that was good enough for me, and well Tee at least, but Jayla was another story. I really didn't expect her to show up. To my surprise she was there before me. She and Tee were sitting on the worn couch chatting it up and laughing like they were the best of friends. I had too much on my mind to pay it much attention.

Emauri was bringing out the last of the refreshments before she sat down and joined us. As soon as her butt hit the chair her doorbell rang. I expected Bree or Danni to come walking through the door, and yet, I was wrong again. Apparently, Emauri had invited one of her friends since it would be the first time we were having hot topics at her place. I huffed when I saw her. It was bad enough that Tee was putting people in the group, now Emauri and on top of everything I wasn't even feeling tonight. So yeah, I huffed, but after the last fiasco, I decided not to act my shoe size.

Emauri introduced us to Summer and she fit the name perfectly. Summer wore her hair in a short sassy style with a vibrant auburn color that reminded me of fresh fallen leaves in fall. She had cute dimples and a soft milk chocolate complexion. Her eyes were bright and bubbly as if she was ready to take on the world. I tilted my head to the side trying to place who she reminded me of, then it dawned on me that she favored the singer, Keyshia Cole.

"Okay," Emauri began, "I think that's everybody so let's begin. My topic of discussion is going to be 'Why do men think it's a crime for older women to date younger men, but it's ok for them to date younger women?'"

I was baffled by the topic for a few reasons. First, it was asking us to evaluate the perspective of a man when we were women which made me think that it was time to open the forum up to men.

"My first thought is why would women date younger?" I asked Emauri, baffled by her question because the thought had never occurred to me to date younger. "It would seem to be only for sex, rarely do you find a younger man that is mature enough for an older woman."

"I would say that some women date younger to see if they still got it, or even get their 'swag' back," Summer said as she did a little dance which immediately told me that she would fit right in with Jayla and Tee.

"I agree with both Summer and Alyssa," Jayla caught me off guard with her comment in agreement with my statement. "But also I've come to the conclusion that it's an ego thing. See they know that whatever they do we can do better. Therefore, they

124

know that young thing is working us like they can't. In other words they're jealous."

I didn't know what to say to Jayla's comment and I still wanted to get to the root of Emauri's statement, so I directed the conversation back to her. "Okay, Emauri. Are we talking mid-life crisis and do women even experience this? I would suppose it crosses genders but I have never heard of such a thing. Summer, you're right I could see people wanting to see if they still got their 'swag', but couldn't they do that with men their own age?"

"Alyssa, it could be mid-life crisis," Emauri admitted. "I myself have been approached by younger men who wanted to start a relationship with me, but when they tell me their age I would tell them I have a daughter their age. Their response to me was 'so what does that mean, age ain't nothing but a number' and me being curious I accept and till this day it's the best sex that I have had in a long time. Plus, this guy helps me with my bills and anything I need for him to do! But I sometimes feel like I'm molesting him, but hey we are grown. Could you be in a relationship like that?"

"Emauri, girl you're not molesting him," Jayla said as she laughed at the thought. "Even though he's younger he's still a grown man. I dated a guy 7 years my junior and as Emauri stated, it was the best sex. At that time in my life my husband and I had separated and it was all about me and what I wanted or needed. From my point of view it was more of a challenge for him rather than me. I was thirty-two with my own house, nice car, two kids, and handling my own, while he was twenty-five living with his mother. He became so clingy, but he also started paying bills so, yes Emauri I have been in a relationship like that. After a year or so, one night after some good sex, I woke him up at 3:00 a.m. telling him he has to go back to momma because sex was really all he could do for me and I realized that wasn't enough."

"I think men just believe that they're the only ones that can get down like that." Tee said, "Alyssa, men take so long to get on our level that it makes no difference if they are 19 or 50, so Emauri, I say get it! Young brothas do a lot of shit that old dudes won't do or can't do."

"Ditto, Tee!" Jayla shouted. "And as we all know by the time we're in our prime at late 30's early 40's most of them are all sexed out."

That made Tee cut a gut-buster laugh as she said, "Jayla, you are crazy but oh so right. I was with this one guy, and this dude couldn't stay hard to save his life."

Like three peas in a pod, Summer began laughing too, "Tee, that is too funny. Alyssa, yes women could do a 'swag' check with men their own age, but it just feels so much better with one that is younger."

"I agree," Tee said, "you do get a better feeling when they are younger."

"Fortunately or unfortunately, however you want to look at it," I said, "I have never been with a younger man in any manner, so that may be why the subject is so foreign to me. As for Emauri's point, I believe that you find a relationship that meets your needs and your standards, the extra stuff is your discretion."

"Tee," Jayla said with an inquisitive expression filing her face. "What was his problem and why didn't you offer him some Viagra? But my question is what's too young? Is there an age limit? I'm asking because I feel some women just go overboard and make themselves look downright stupid. Also, just because they're younger are they not expected to be a man other than in the bed?"

"Wow, Jays, you said a mouthful. I think there is no age limit. If that person makes you feel the way you want to feel then it doesn't matter. I would not care how it made me look. If we based everything we did on the way it looked to others we might as well throw in the towel. Someone is always gonna have something to say about whatever we do."

"I think a lot of times," Tee continued "when men or women do younger, I don't believe they care a whole lot about how they act as a man or a woman, they are more interested in what they putting on them in the bedroom. To answer your question Jays, I don't know what he was taking or not taking...all I know is my girl was highly disappointed."

We chatted a little longer about nothing in particular. I broached the subject of having men included in our next meeting; everyone seemed excited about the idea. I began thinking of ways to make it come to fruition.

Q WAS SLOWLY...

making me remember why I fell in love with him. He was saying everything I needed to hear and because of that I didn't trust him. As much as my heart wanted to, my mind told me to run the other way. I didn't want to give up on eight years, but I didn't want to stay and wind up wishing I had left. I still hadn't discussed Tiffany's visit to my home with him. Right now, I was just enjoying being a woman who had a handsome man vying for her attention. I didn't want to ruin that moment bringing up what or who doesn't matter.

"Hello."

"Can I speak to Alyssa?"

"Q, who else is going to answer my phone?"

"I don't know, you could have mama and 'em over or something. It could be one of your hot topic nights, who knows?"

"Answering my cell phone and at this hour?" I looked over at the clock that read 11:45 p.m. I stretched. I had been lying in my bed catching up on a few good reads when he phoned. "And what do you know about hot topics anyways."

"I know a lot. What you guys meet like once a month right?"

"Yes."

"I bet y'all be in there doing a lot of male bashing."

129

"As a matter of fact we don't. We really try to give a lot of food for thought, you know, iron sharpening iron. Now if men come up under the gun in our conversations you have no one else to blame but yourselves," I said with a light laugh.

"That's what your mouth say. What you should do is open the floor for some men to get in on it."

"Do you have a bug on me or something?"

"No, why do you say that?"

"Because, in all of the years that we have been having the conversations, not once have we ever thought to include men until the last session. Now all of a sudden you're showing an interest in it."

"I'm showing an interest in you, but if that's an open invitation, I'll take it."

"Hold up, I didn't get that far yet."

"Okay, well how about this, how about you let me take you out tomorrow and if you have a good time then you'll let me come and if you don't I'll stay in the dog house."

"Sounds like a fair challenge, okay. What time?"

"11:30"

"That's an early date."

"Yeah, I wouldn't want to keep you out too late."

"Okay, good night."

"Wait, I wasn't done with the conversation."

"I was; if you have me getting ready for an early date, then I need to get some beauty sleep. I can't have you seeing me all jacked-up."

"Oh, I've already seen that."

"Shut up!" I laughed, "I'm hanging up now."

"Okay, lovely lady, you have a good night."

I felt giddy and excited. I couldn't wait to see Q tomorrow. I smiled into my pillow, feeling the same exhilaration that I had when we first met.

HE WAS BACK...

at the free clinic to get his results. He wanted to get his results and never look back at this place again. One thing he knew for sure was that he would never have unprotected sex of any sort after this. Well, almost never, he thought to himself as he knew how unrealistic that feat was for him. There were too many times that he found himself in unpredictable situations that he just couldn't pass on.

He had told Alyssa what she wanted to hear. What man wouldn't? He darn sure wasn't going to be honest enough to tell her what his sex life really looked like.

"Mr. Thomas, the doctor will see you now," the nurse said.

"Thank you," he said as he stood and walked toward her so that she could lead him to the office for his consult. He had been calling himself Anthony Thomas for the past three days. He didn't want to forget the bogus name he had put down neither did he want the embarrassing occurrence that happened the last time he was there. So this time when she called him, he was prepared.

"Have a seat, Mr. Thomas" the doctor instructed. "Seems we have been quite active," she said as he sat down.

"I don't follow."

"I'm not sure what you expected us to find, but I strongly recommend that you slow down."

"Are you going to give me my results or a spiritual counseling?"

"I'm sorry, you must be anxious. Okay, let's see here," she said as she opened his file and glanced over it. "You had some concerns about the HSV virus, commonly known as Herpes. Your results show that you have been exposed to both HSV1 and 2."

"What does that mean?"

"Well, HSV1 is oral and HSV2 is genital. Exposure merely means that it is showing in your blood, however, we don't need to begin treatment until you begin showing outward symptoms. Have you had a breakout of any sort yet?"

"No."

"Have you been experiencing any other symptoms, cold sores, itching, or soreness?"

"No," he said as he shook his head disappointed that his sexual habits had caught up with him in the worse way. He didn't want to deal with this. He had hoped that he could make it through life without ever facing any STD. "Is that all?"

"Actually, no" she said as she looked up from her chart. "It appears you have Chlamydia as well."

"What!" he shouted as he stood up from his seat. "I was coming in here thinking you were going to give me a clean bill of health, but you're sitting there telling me, I have not one but three different infections. How in the hell could I have three infections, I don't have any symptoms."

"Mr. Thomas, I am going to need you to either sit down and calm down or leave my office. I didn't give you the infections, I gave you the news."

"You're right, I'm sorry. It's just so much to take in at once."

"I understand, but I will not allow you to have outbursts like this in my office. They're uncalled for."

"I understand."

"As I was saying, both Chlamydia and Herpes can go undetected because many times people experience no signs at all, or it can lay dormant until your immune system weakens. I will write you a prescription for antibiotics and that should clear up the Chlamydia within 5 – 10 days. Unfortunately, there isn't a cure for Herpes, but if you start experiencing outbreaks or other symptoms we can prescribe medication that will help with those. Okay?" she said as she tore the paper from her pad and handed it to him.

"Thanks," he mumbled as he took the paper and stood to walk out of the free clinic that opened the door to a very traumatic time in his life.

"Mr. Thomas, I know you don't want to hear this but it could be worse."

"It can't be any worse than this for me."

"Actually, it could be. Your HIV results came back negative, and that's a good thing. Think of all the people whose tests didn't. Unfortunate as it may be, this doesn't necessarily mean that you don't have the virus. So a word of advice, wrap it up. Safe sex really is the best sex. You can determine how to define safe, but I caution you to let your definition line up. I don't want to see you in here for something that really could be worse."

"What do you mean I may still have the virus? The HIV virus?"

"Yes. You have to keep yourself protected over a course of two years, coming back every six months for testing. Once you've tested negative for a complete two years without exposing yourself, then you're clear."

135

He shook his head before continuing his journey out the door.

"Mr. Thomas," she said just as his hand touched the door knob, he turned and faced her.

"Yes."

"Maybe you would like some of these," she said as she held a handful of condoms toward him.

"No, thank you. I use Magnum, those things never work," he said almost boastfully, yet unintentionally.

I Had Told...

Q that I needed to get some beauty sleep, however, I couldn't sleep a wink. I was like a kid the night before Christmas, anxious and excited. The fact that Q thought enough of our marriage to really put an effort in the right direction, made me feel beautiful again.

I flipped through the clothes in my closet trying to find the perfect outfit. I had to give him a glimpse of who he had walked away from. I had been in the closet for a half an hour and nothing seemed to have the meaning that I wanted to convey. Either he had seen it too many times or it wasn't the right color, whatever the reason I wasn't happy with my selections.

I walked out and looked at the night stand it was 8:30, the mall opened at 9:00. I gave thought to running out and buying something new, but quickly threw that idea out. Q would be there in 3 hours and I knew that it would be just as hard for me to find something there as it was for me finding something in my own wardrobe. Besides, I couldn't let Q know that I was feeling him tough enough to buy a new outfit for the occasion. So back to my closet I go. I closed my eyes trying to refresh my mind before I stared at the same clothes again.

I hadn't even asked where we were going, although I doubted that he would say if I did. So, I thought about what I could wear that would fit in anywhere. I decided on my long white sundress with faces printed in black covering it and my black half sweater.

Q arrived a few minutes early, all smiles. It was contagious, I smiled with him.

"You look beautiful, Alyssa."

"You don't look so bad either, mister."

"Shall we?" he said as he held his hand out for me. Again, I was impressed. I assumed he was going to come in and chat or something, but apparently Q was really treating this like our first date. Q wore black slacks and a black V-neck fitted shirt. I felt comfortable in my choice.

"So, where are we going?" I asked as I slid into Q's passenger seat.

"It's an ancient Chinese secret," Q said as he closed my door. It had been awhile since he opened my door for me. I smiled but it quickly faded as I remembered that this too may pass as it did once before.

Q noticed the change in my expression when he got in the car.

"What happened?"

"Nothing."

"Alyssa, don't do this. One thing I've learned from you is that communication is a must, and with that communication must come honesty. Now, I can clearly see something is wrong, so what is it?"

"What are we doing, Q? We have gone down this road before, why are we revisiting it?"

"Because I love you, and I need us to start from the beginning so we can find out where we went wrong."

"We don't need to go back to do that, I can tell you right now."

"Alyssa, please don't do this. Clear your mind of past mistakes, let's choose to learn from them rather than harbor on them."

I smiled.

"See, that's what I'm talking about, I knew you had it in you."

"Maybe just a little," I said as I squinted my eye and pinched my fingers together.

"A little is all I need," Q said as he drove off. We arrived at the Aquarium and I frowned a little. That didn't make it past Q either. "Alyssa, I need you to work with me."

"I'm working, I'm working," I said as I shook all negative thoughts from my mind.

The Aquarium was more beautiful than I had expected it to be. I was in awe of the whales; the whole scene was simply breathtaking. I was happy that the hammerhead sharks were behind the thick glass. I walked so close to the glass my nose was seconds from touching it. Just as the shark got close, Q touched both my sides and I jumped, my forehead hit the glass.

I laughed and turned to hit him, but he wrapped his arms around my waist and gave me a small kiss on the lips. It was nice. I had forgotten how soft his lips were.

"Gotcha," he mouthed as he took my hand and we finished our tour. 'Yeah, you got me in more ways than one,' I thought to myself. It was way too early for Q to know he had me open.

When we got back to the car, I stood by the passenger door waiting for Q to open it, but instead he walked on the other side of the car. I rolled my eyes and mumbled, "that didn't last long." I tried to snatch the door open but it was locked. I huffed, crossed my arms then leaned against the door waiting for him.

He didn't get in on the driver's side; he opened the trunk and pulled out a picnic basket. I felt foolish and was thankful that Q hadn't caught my mini tantrum.

"So what do you have in there, that's been sitting for so long?" I asked as I frowned my face.

Q shut the trunk, "I'll have you know, this just got in here. I know people, thank you very much, and what's in here is for me to know..."

"And me to find out," I finished his sentence as I lunged for the picnic basket to no avail. Q was quicker than I was.

"Aught, aught, aught," Q said as he placed the basket behind his back and waved his index finger at me.

That little finger wasn't going to stop me, as I walked up to him sexily. "Q," I sang, "what's in the basket?" When I reached him, he grabbed me by the waist and planted another kiss on me, this one made me forget what I was after.

"You'll find out in a moment," he said as he walked me to the park that was near the aquarium. We sat on one of the benches near the waterfall. Q placed the basket in between us, yet away from me. I tried peeking around and every time I did, he would turn it away. I gave up trying; the game had lost its flavor.

He pulled out a small bottle of hand sanitizer and handed it to me. "What, you think you know me," I said as I took it and sanitized my hands.

"We're about to find out aren't we, he said as he pulled out a Subway sandwich and closed the basket. He sanitized his hands then opened the sandwich and gave me half.

"Are you serious?"

"What?"

"You went through all that fuss for a Subway sandwich?"

"No, you went through all of that fuss; I'm just trying to feed you."

"So where are the chocolate covered strawberries, the exotic cheeses and bottle of wine?"

"You don't like strawberries, you rarely drink wine or at least in the past you rarely drank you're on the verge of an alcoholic now." Q said as he laughed at his own joke.

"Ha, ha, very funny," I said not amused the least. He was right, I had been dabbling a little more in the wine bottle, but it wasn't a laughing matter. "What about the cheese?"

"There's cheese on the sandwich," Q said as he raised his sandwich like a toast, "now let's eat."

"Whatever," I said knowing that he was right on all points. I bit into my sandwich and was in heaven it was so good. Q opened the basket and pulled out an ice cold Pepsi. "You're pulling out all the stops aren't you?" I said as I took the Pepsi.

"The sky's the limit for you baby, the sky's the limit."

"So, where do you think we went wrong?"

"I think we lost our direction a couple times down the road, but the key is in understanding that. Remembering to cherish the one you love and not take them for granted."

"Yeah, you sure did take me for granted; I still think it was because you never thought that I would leave."

"Uh, actually, Alyssa, I think we took one another for granted. This road is a two-way street. You got just as comfortable with me as I did you. There were a whole lot of things that you stopped doing. Coming home was no longer fun. I felt like I was always coming home to a headache, hence the reason for the apartment. I had to have some place that I could come home and just have peace."

"I can understand that."

"What? No argument from the great debater."

"No," I said as I waved my white napkin, "I surrender."

"And for that, I will let you have dessert," he said as he reached into the basket and pulled out one Hershey's chocolate bar with almonds.

"For me," I said as I placed my hand on my chest as if I was being awarded the Nobel Peace Prize. "Where's yours?" I asked as I bit into the bar.

"I was kind of hoping we would share."

"Oh no, my brother, you have got to get your own," I said and bit into the bar again. "Ummmm, it's so good too, so many almonds. Q walked over to me and began tickling my sides, I burst into laughter. "Okay, okay, you're going to make me choke," I said as I gave him the bar.

It was a wonderful afternoon date. Q drove me home and walked me to the door. The happy expression that he had the entire day had turned solemn. I assumed it was because our date was coming to an end. I was kind of bummed about it too.

"Listen, Lyss, I had a wonderful day with you, but I think there's something we need to talk about before we go any further."

"I don't too much like the sound of this, Q."

"I didn't either when I first heard it, but I'd rather you hear it from me, than through the rumor mill."

"Okay, then I will, but not today Q. Everything has been so perfect, let's not ruin it with talk that will change that, okay?"

"Okay," he said as he kissed me on the forehead. Even though it was daylight still, Q waited until I got into the house before he turned and walked away.

142

ALYSSA HAD GIVEN...

him nothing but honesty, even when honesty was the hardest to do. He still remembered her face as she announced to everyone in the room that she was now exposed to herpes. He felt it was a brave move. For this he felt it was only right to return the favor, as much as he didn't want to.

He didn't know if she was his origin, or he was hers, but at this point none of that mattered. He rubbed his hand across his face as he contemplated the different ways that he could tell her. Nothing he thought of made sense. It was a bitter pill to swallow no matter how he looked at it. The doorbell rang and pulled him out of his thoughts.

He wasn't expecting anyone, so he thought it was a little strange. Maybe it was Jehovah Witness he said as he swung his door without even asking who it was or peering through the hole. He couldn't understand why he never followed his first mind. She was the last person he wanted to see right now.

"How can I help you?"

"Can I come in?"

"Is it necessary?"

"I know you have more class than to have a personal conversation out in public?"

"Right, the same class you have to come by unannounced. So what is it, Tiffany?"

"I know you don't believe me, but I'm pregnant and the baby is yours."

He dropped his head, some women were relentless, and Tiffany was one of them. He moved to the side and allowed her to enter his apartment.

FACEBOOK MADE MY TASK...

of finding men to include in our group much easier. I glared at the post as I read it again for the 5th time.

> Do you really have the audacity to believe that I would need to ask you for sex? Apparently, you took no notice to the way I looked at you, for you to believe that I am that shallow. To be perfectly honest, I am not attracted to you physically but mentally. Don't blame me because you're so into yourself that you want to put me in a barrel with every other man and think that I too, want a piece of you. Let me ask you this, have you ever even fathomed the possibility that a man could want you for more than just sex? Have you ever even tried having a relationship that didn't consist of the physical? You have me second thinking my attraction, because somewhere along the line, either I misunderstood you or you misunderstood me, but the bottom line is this, I would never ask you for sex, because for me that would be something we would mutually give to the other.

I contacted the author because he had my mind wide open with intrigue. The depth and urgency in his writing willed me to know more about him, and if I knew the ladies like I thought I did,

I knew they would be just as intrigued. I sent the message to them so they could ponder over it and give me some feedback. I wondered if anyone would be offended and then quickly pushed past that thought because I realized that it didn't matter.

If we were really trying to educate our minds and move to another level then some offense may take place, but the growth in the end will make it worth it. Jayla was the first to respond, she sent me a text.

> Ok then! That surely woke me up this morning when I saw the first line rolling across my phone. :-)

I responded back,

> It did the same for me, which is why I had to share it with the group. Then after reading further and seeing the depth from which he came, it became a must share. It brushes on the same topics we have, but from a man's perspective.

> Uh yeah...it is rather deep. Really looking forward to see what the men have to say.

Tee's text came behind hers,

> Yes I like this very much.

Followed by Emauri's,

> O wow.... This is going to be a very deep discussion that I'm going to love!!!!

Apparently, our forum intrigued Jackson as much as he intrigued us. He agreed to meet with us and discuss the motivation behind this writing. Everyone was ready for this topic, well everyone except Q. He had been trying hard to put our marriage back on track, and I respected that. I also respected the fact that I could not bring another man in the house again, so we were meeting at Tee's and because Jackson would be there I invited Q. To my surprise he accepted.

"Okay, Tee" I said after everyone had arrived and found their place of comfort. "I know this is your spot, but if you don't mind, I would like to get this one started."

"Do you, I don't trip over small shit like that."

"Jackson," I said as I tried not to smile too hard, being cognizant of the fact that Q was watching my every move, "please share with us your motivation for a statement so bold and so insightful. The opening really catches you off guard and makes you stop, but if you read on, you read the depth in this message and the respect you have for women. Do you feel that men have more respect for women then we have for ourselves?"

Jackson was tall and thin, frail almost, he wore his clothes way too big for him, but somehow he made it work. His aura was strong, so he had everyone's attention. He was dark skinned and bald. His eyes spoke volumes, they were piercing and deep, as was his voice, although to hear him speak took away from the intelligence he held vastly. Although the words he said held our attention, I couldn't get past the street slur he had, which broke his words and made some of them barely audible.

"I wouldn't and couldn't say if men have more respect for women then they have for themselves. I can only speak to what type of man I am. I believe a lot of times women may be quick to jump to that conclusion meaning a man is trying to get at them for a sexual purpose and being slick about it. That type of behavior and pre-judgment is what lead to that statement. Take a chance to get to know me as you want me to know you and once you do take proper notice in me you will see I'm much deeper than just trying to get in your pants. I am much deeper than that. My mental has to be stimulated for me to even be interested in your physical."

"I wonder if the pre-judgment comes from past experience" I said feeling as if I was interviewing him, "and if that's the case, does the ball fall back to the court of the men. It is wonderful that you spoke on behalf of you versus men as a whole, but the insight you have speaks so profoundly for true men."

"Before you answer that," Tee said, "I want to make sure that I understand you correctly. Are you saying that your initial reason for approaching a woman is not to get in her panties? I thought the first appeal is the physical."

"Tee," Q said, "I think you're missing the point of what he is saying here. Some women have a pre-conceived notion that men are always trying to run game to get the goodies, yet through my experiences I've seen women run this game much smoother than a man to their benefit. Why must this game be played to conquer one another by the slickest means necessary?"

"It's reasons why women feel as we do, because in most cases men are trying to run game for the goodies," Jayla answered before Tee and I again, I took note to how much alike they really were. "Also, most men are attracted to our physical before they even find out what type of mind we have. Yes Q, women have a much tighter game but that's because men are so weak to the flesh that when we either say what you all want to hear or do something to turn you all on, the top head gets turned off and you all are led by the other one, but to answer your question, no one wants to be 'played' therefore everyone plays again until they get to see one another for who and what they really are."

As Jayla saw that all eyes were on her, she took over the floor, and I got the feeling that she loved every moment of it.

"Now," she continued as she moved to the edge of her seat, "Jackson said that his mental has to be stimulated for him to be interested in a woman's physical. I don't know you, so I have to take you for your word." She looked directly at Jackson as if to challenge his version of what was true, "I would think that kind of stands for most men in a way. In other words, he'll hit it from the start but if her mental is on point he'll keep her around. Whereas if not then it's just a sex thing. Nowadays, men don't wait too long for a woman to get to know him before she gives it up simply because he doesn't have to, because there are plenty of women who will. That doesn't mean you won't keep pursuing that other woman but in the meantime more likely than none, you're being sexually satisfied by someone else."

"Oh wow, Jayla" Emauri said. "You hit it right on the nail and took the words right out of my mouth. But what I want to know as it pertains to Jayla's statement; is it difficult for a man to see a woman with a male because they all know the games they pulled on women?"

"I believe that both women and men love playing the game because the excitement is in the catch," Tee said, "and once the catching has ended, both men and women, mostly men, find it hard to stay around."

Jackson looked at me as if I had walked him into a ticking time bomb. I took a sip of my Pepsi and waited to hear what he would say to the many statements that had been thrown his way.

"Okay," he said as he slapped his hands on his thighs and moved them to his knees as if he was wiping sweat from his palms. "Jayla, what I was stating was not that I would hit it from the front and keep her around if she stimulates my mental. I couldn't even begin to think about hitting it unless my mental has already been stimulated. Women are so infatuated with themselves that they think that all men want them for is sex, but I tend to wonder if they ever offered their mind. My statement is not to say I would hit it, it is to show that the woman within herself is being shallow and had I met her in that place we would be wading in the midst of deception on both our parts. However I am more inclined to decline the unannounced offer of sex to display my disappointment and loss of respect for any and all women who practice this principle of thinking all men are not thinking beyond their waist."

"Wow, Jackson," I said as I literally exhaled after his spiel. It felt like I was holding my breath hanging on to his every word. "Do you feel like you are a rarity amongst Black men?" I watched as Q became visibly tense at my question, that was not my intention.

"I feel I am of unique character by any standards or race concerning man. I also feel most women have a pre-assumed ideal on all men especially the men in their race."

"Can anyone answer this question for me," Emauri began, "Do men and women date each other anymore before they have sex?"

"Of course they do," Jackson answered, "which is what my statement is about, getting to really know a person."

"I have to disagree with you, Jackson" I said. "I believe this is another thing that is exclusive to men of your standard. You are of a unique character by any standards. Emauri, this is a discussion that Tee and I were just having, dating has become obsolete."

"Jackson, you have me curious to know how do you normally meet women? What I would also love to hear from you is if you have a description of the ideal woman?" Again Q gave me a look that made me feel awkward. Something told me that he would have this reaction. He wasn't quite ready to venture this deep into our relationship. However, I felt if we were really going to give our marriage a fighting chance, we needed to conquer trust one day at a time. I was pleased that he didn't just act a complete fool in front of everyone. In fact, I think only Tee and I noticed his discomfort.

"It seems to me that dating is obsolete," Emauri responded "because every time I'm approached by a man it's always about sex I really had to reevaluate myself and see if my personality was giving mix signals as an easy prey, target or a good woman with high standards."

"Emauri, I'm not trying to stop the flow of what you're saying, but Jackson got me tripping." Tee said, "Jackson, are you saying that a woman is shallow if she automatically assumes that a man wants to sleep with her? Is that being shallow or is that just being real about a situation. I would love for a man to just want to talk and get to know Tee. I would love to talk to a man and have him feed me, mentally."

"Yes it is shallow. Very in fact, you wouldn't think so? I mean if a woman can only view men in this light what does that say about her really? You can only be fed when you have an appetite that stretches beyond the man wanting you for sex."

"Wow!" Jayla said, "I can't believe your answers Jackson. Let me get my thoughts straight and get back with you."

"What? I hope you don't feel disrespected." Jackson said with a look of astonishment as he took a sip of his drink and placed it gently back on the coaster.

"Oh no, nothing like that just give me a minute."

"Okay."

"Jackson" I began trying to give words to Jayla's emotions as well as mine, perhaps a few others in the room. "I think we are all floored by your answers in a good way, which is why I feel extremely blessed that you agreed to be in this forum, you are doing exactly what I needed, giving much food for thought."

"Maybe I can place man in a better light for you ladies. I have a straight forward approach and I am very honest, Alyssa. To address your earlier question, I couldn't describe for you the ideal woman, because the ideal woman has no real description she is just that ideal. She meets all criteria's of a woman with understanding. She is a great lover, a great communicator, and a great representation to all women. She's the type of woman that other women look at and openly admire and secretly want to be her."

"Ok, Jackson enough of the bullshit," Jayla blurted sounding every bit of Tee. "Now what makes Tee's question so far-fetched? How are we shallow if we think about a man wanting to sleep with us? Maybe we should just take you, as a man, out of the equation and only talk about other men in the world. Just as Emauri stated about her having to step back and evaluate herself simply because every time we step out some man is all up in our space. Well a lot of us have done that because of the bold disrespectful comments. We can't help if we're attractive with desirable attributes, that's just who we are. And what about this line "Can we at least be friends?" Ugggggh! I just told you I'm not interested but they keep trying. So, does that mean we're somehow misrepresenting ourselves? Please explain. What is it about you that make you different that you're not physically attracted to a woman initially by sight? I'm all ears."

"Well what makes me different than the average man that is going off of the woman's physical is just that. I need to know your thoughts before I can desire your body, because if you are dumb witted I won't be able to tolerate you as a woman attractive physically or not. I'm the guy that's quiet in the room until someone says something that piques my interest. Tee's question was shallow within itself. She asked do I think that a woman is shallow if she thinks a man is only out to get in her panties? Of course I do, just as shallow as a woman thinks a man is for doing so. Tee also said that she thought the physical was the first attraction which says to me if she doesn't find a man attractive then she won't even bother to listen to him period because her mind won't allow it. You put a title on it."

"Ladies, ladies, ladies," I said mocking Nephew Tommy from Steve Harvey's morning show. "I have to say that I want to unite with you guys, God knows I do, but Jackson is hitting this thing straight out of the ball park. We have to start looking at what we're accepting and understanding therein lies the problem."

"True, Alyssa." Jackson said and I smiled as if I had just gotten the right answer and the professor was giving me accolades for it.

Q had been listening quietly I assumed he was collecting his thoughts. Knowing Q, I knew he was not going to be outdone by another man in the presence of his wife, sister and their friends, so he listened and waited for his opportunity to feed our minds as well. As if on cue, he spoke.

"Emauri," Q started his spiel, "to answer your question, dating has become obsolete compared to the days of old to really go through the process of courtship. Look at what we have today, speed-dating, Skype, texting, sexting, brief conversations - how can you begin to know a person through these outlets, much less gain respect for one another. I pose this question: What are you really looking for reality or fairytale? Some women have a secret agenda, they want this ideal or flawless guy that can wow them and stimulate their intellect, yet they will accept being disrespected and treated like less than the Queen that they are for the infatuation of being with a thug to turn them out. The guys are not exempt, they want this flawless woman with little challenge but on the real they want the woman to be submissive while he treats her like a freak and dogs her out, so again I pose, what are you really looking for?"

"Hmmm, Quan" Jackson started with his eyebrow raised. "I must disagree with you about what men really want. In fact most men really want their woman not to be submissive but more to the woman's character and that is a nurturer that is a woman's natural order you can see that through the process of life. Who carries the seed? Who has the natural ability to care for the seed? A true man is always looking for a woman that can provide growth to his character. The true challenge is not on the woman but the man to exhibit traits that will make the woman reflective of him in the sense of their relationship so that all others outside can clearly see that they are really one instead of two."

I was excited about Jackson's words; he seemed to understand the true depth of a woman. Obviously, I had to tread softly so I remained silent, listening intently.

"I'll give you that, Jackson" Q agreed and I was so pleased, "you make a valid point and I see the attributes displayed in the older and mature generation. I'm from the old school and I believe a woman should be treated with the utmost respect. My hat's off to all of the strong Black women who continue to be the backbone of the family. It's sad to see this younger generation disrespect one another on a crazy level. There's no true love displayed, only what's the term now "associates" no commitment just sex and on to the next."

"Very true," Jackson commented. "However, I must say that is due to the grooming of the youth today not just in the area of male and female relationships but all relationships they encounter."

"I want to comment on our earlier conversation, Jackson," Tee said. "First of all, I don't think that my statement is shallow at all. You said that you can't be attracted to someone's physical until you get into their mind. I have to say sir you are one in a million. When God made you He made you extremely different. I can see how you can say that you won't be sexual with someone until you first get to know that person, but to not be physically attracted to that person before talking to her, is crazy to me.

I guess my confusion comes into play when you said you have to hear someone talk first and if they interest you, I guess that's when you approach this person? I'm trying to find out in what type of environment do you meet this person, because the only setting that I can see is at some type of dinner party. I honestly think that you are not being totally truthful.

You are telling me that you NEVER in your life approached a woman based on her beauty, her smile, her eyes, her butt. There are so many songs based on just that thing, I'm not talking about rap songs either. I'm talking about beautiful love songs, so for you to say that my question is shallow, I beg to differ, there are too many men out there who I have heard say that they have to be physically attracted to a woman in order for them to approach her, so we can agree to disagree."

"The men you speak of and the music you speak of are calling out to an audience that is known to exist. How I can meet these people are simple. Through observance, body language speaks volumes as an ice breaker. How many times have you been heading in one person's direction and suddenly changed gears as you were advancing to someone that may seem to be more helpful. Or just saw a man walk in a room and assume his position in life because of how he carries himself? I'm not saying I won't be sociable with people in any setting but to just look at someone and immediately find purpose for attraction is shallow and also the main ingredient in a bad relationship that usually ends bad because the beginning was baseless."

"Tee, I have to disagree with you," I said. "I think that you can be attracted to a person's mind way before you are attracted to them physically. I can attest to several relationships that I have had based on this very thing. I agree that people are always vying for the physical, so much so that they force themselves to be in relationships that are unhealthy for them mentally and sometimes very abusive. I think that people should reevaluate their reason for a relationship."

"I don't know if it's just me that's just not getting it. It seems like we are off the subject," Tee responded. "Jackson, the point was that you said you are not physically attracted to a woman, you are only attracted to her mind not her body, so I asked how do you meet these people and you say through their body language, I'm confused. Alyssa, these relationships you speak of, these men approached you, you didn't approach them, so how do you know that they didn't approach you based on what you had behind you?" Tee said referring to my more than ample behind, which I took a slight offense to. I feel like I have a whole lot more to offer to a relationship than my backside.

"Tee, body language and physical attraction are two entirely different things correct? Can someone not summon you by curling their finger and motioning toward you? I read people through their movements. Your actions rarely ever betray the truth of your character."

I was in complete awe of Jackson. His way of thinking was rare amongst men of any race and I prayed that there would come a day that we would have more of him and less of the ones that the ladies were describing. I understood the argument on both ends, but the growth that I walked away with today was more to Jackson's point. I walked away understanding that no matter what relationship I was in, I needed to understand that it was all about what I was willing to accept.

I RODE WITH Q...

to the meeting. The drive home was really changing things for me. Q was being so attentive and loving. I was having thoughts of giving him some tonight. His input during tonight's hot topic conversation fed my appetite in more ways than one. Yeah, I was feeling Q again in a real good way.

"So what did you think of your first conversation?"

"It was interesting."

"Would you do it again?"

"Maybe."

"What is with all these short answers? Is everything okay?"

"Just got a lot on my mind."

"Is it something I did or said?" I asked feeling that maybe things hadn't changed as much as I thought they did. Q was giving me the same brush off that he had given me the first night that Ahmad called.

"No."

"Is this about Jackson?" I asked.

"No," he answered as he let his hand rest on mine easing the tension some. "Do you remember after our date, I told you that I needed to talk to you about some things?"

"Yeah Q, I remember. I just don't know if our relationship can withstand the type of conversation that you obviously want to have."

"So what do we do, just keep running from the conversation? Alyssa, I love you more than life itself, that's never going to change. I want us to get to a point where you feel the same way."

"I never stopped loving you, Q."

"Okay, then why can't we talk about anything without fear that we will end our relationship? We said for better or worse, and I mean it. I got a little off track, but I'm here to stick this thing out now, and nothing you can say to me will have me walk out of your life," he said as he momentarily took his eyes off the road to meet mine.

"Baby, we've already had one heavy conversation for the night. I have a plan, how about I cook you dinner tomorrow night and we can talk then," I said wanting this conversation to be over. It was ruining the peaceful drive home that I thought we would have. I liked the fact that Q was becoming a better communicator. That was definitely a great start, but I just didn't like what he wanted to say.

Everything in me was telling me that his conversation had to do with one of two things or both. Tiffany's pregnancy or him having herpes and I was not in the mood to hear either right now. I turned on the radio and let the smooth sounds of the jazz station change the atmosphere.

"Q," I sang as I danced in my seat. "You know what we should do?"

"What's that?" he said as he smiled in my direction and the tension eased a little more.

"We should go dancing. You know, the Chicago-style step, type dancing."

"You up for it?"

"I am," I said as I looked at him sensuously telling him I was up for a whole lot more than that.

"What the lady asks, she shall receive," Q said smiling widely as he turned the car around and headed to the club.

Yeah, we were definitely heading in the right direction.

THE SOUND OF MY...

cell phone going off was disturbing the sleep that I so desperately wanted right now. I looked at the clock and saw that it was a little after eight. Q had just dropped me back at the house not even four hours ago. We had shut the club down. Afterward, we went to grab something to eat because all of that dancing gave us both a hearty appetite.

I smiled as I remembered the night we had. The cell phone went off again; reminding me why I was woke when I didn't want to be. I picked it up and saw Ahmad's picture on the screen. I put the phone back down, there was nothing that I wanted to talk to him about again ever in life.

I rolled back over and attempted to go back to sleep. Not having to punch anyone's clock anymore had its perks and this was definitely one of them.

My phone went off again, again I picked it up and Ahmad's picture was on the display. I pressed ignore and sent him straight to voicemail. A minute or two later I heard it beep which meant he had left a message. I sighed aloud and placed the pillow over my head. Another beep, someone had sent a text.

I picked up the phone and put it on silent, put it under the pillow beside me and drifted back off to sleep. After another two hours, my body was satisfied. I stretched all of the kinks out of my lower back and legs and felt refreshed. That was followed by a yawn which was followed by the loud ringing of the house phone causing my eyes to snap open.

I rubbed the sleep from my eyes and got up to get the phone, but by the time I reached it the caller had hung up. I turned to walk away but it rang again almost immediately. I looked at the caller ID, it was Tee.

"What up?" I answered.

"You, heifer, you can't seem to answer your phone no more. What you and Q sleeping in?"

"I'm sleeping in. I don't know what Q is doing."

"Uh huh, y'all look cute being back together smiling and shit. I just assumed he would have been all up in that with the way y'all were carrying on."

"Whatever, Tee." I smiled because before the conversation during our drive home, that's exactly what I was thinking too. "So, Q has some heavy conversation that he must have with me and I'm thinking it has something to do with the fact that Tiffany is pregnant or he wants to confess that he too has been exposed to herpes."

"What is exposed? Either you have that shit or you don't."

"Yeah, I agree, but exposed just makes it sound a little better, for me at least. I mean until I actually have a breakout. Which I'm praying never happens, because I'm not ready to deal with that."

"And what the hell you gone do if old girl is pregnant with Q's baby?"

"Take one day at a time, breathe in, breathe out."

"Great job, kid. Looks like you're growing up the hard way, the long way, but you're doing it and I am proud of you."

"Awww, Big Sister, almighty! I couldn't have done it without you being such a constant in my life."

"So, why aren't you answering your cell?"

"Oh, dang. I completely forgot about that. Ahmad was trying to reach me while I was trying to get some sleep, so I put it on silent."

"Ooooooh, sounds like you still trying to have your cake and eat it too."

"Tee, you know I hate that saying, who want's cake just to look at it? But no, I'm good on Ahmad. He has shown me in more ways than one, that he is not the man I hyped him up to be."

"Really, Alyssa? Has he shown you that or is that what you want to believe because that's what's easier."

"Tee, the stuff that he's been saying to me," I started before Tee cut me off.

"Says that he is a man who is hurt, a man who would love nothing more than to be with you but knowing your situation he can't. So yeah, he pushes you away so he won't draw you closer and now you're throwing him to the wolves like he's all bad."

"I'm not throwing him anywhere. He is where he's at because that's where he put himself. Come on, Tee. You know better than anyone else that I tried with Ahmad. I was feeling him tougher than I wanted to."

"Too tough!" Tee said as she laughed wickedly.

"Oh whatever, Tee. You get my point."

"I get it, but do you. Sounds to me like you still have some decisions that need to be made."

"Actually, I don't. I have decided what's best for me is to let life take its course and just prepare myself for the ride."

Tee and I talked for at least an hour. It was good having a sister that I can also call a confidant and a friend. I scratched my head as I realized that Tee almost always listened more than she ever talked. She advised us well most times but who was there for Tee.

Seafood Salad...

macaroni and cheese, broccoli, corn bread muffins and turkey
meatloaf was the best I could muster for dinner tonight. It really
was a combination of the things I made best. I didn't want to go
with the traditional steak and potatoes, so I winged it. I looked
over the table that I had eloquently designed and stuck my chest
out. "I think I did pretty well if I can say so myself." I said out
loud to myself.

"All of this for me," Carnell said as he came down and looked
over the table licking his lips.

"No, how about, none of this is for you."

"See, that's what I'm talking about, you don't ever feed me
this good."

"Don't start telling lies," I said as both Carnell and I broke
into laughter. "Your sister is on her way to pick you up. You and
she are hanging out tonight."

"Did anyone think to ask Carnell, what Carnell wanted to do?"

"I hate when you talk about yourself in third person, but no we
didn't ask you because it didn't matter. Your dad and I are in need
of some serious private time tonight, so you don't get a say in the
matter."

"Step-dad"

"So you're still mad huh."

Carnell looked down at his feet; sadness covered him for a moment. He and Q's relationship had been declining more and more lately. I continued to pray that they would make things right. Although, Carnell had a relationship with his father, it was so minimal that I barely wanted to give it credit as a relationship. Q was the first man to really step into his life and be a father, but as we began bumping heads so did they.

Carnell smiled and kissed me on my cheek, "If you're happy, I'm happy, but please be genuinely happy, ma."

"I will be," I said assuring him that I had my head on straight now.

"Okay, I'm gone head up and get ready to get out of here. Did she say where we we're going."

"I think skating and a movie, of course y'all will be grabbing a bite to eat while you're out too."

"Cool," he said as he dashed off and was gone just as quickly as he came.

The doorbell rang shortly after Carnell left with his sister. Q wore a brown "pimp daddy" hat with some sexy brown slacks and a silk brown button-up, striped brown Stacy Adams completed his attire. When I opened the door he had his head in his chest so that all I could see was the top of his hat.

"Come on in, Mr. Suave," I said as I walked back toward the kitchen, "and leave the hat. You just messed up a good hook-up."

"What, you don't like my hat? I thought hats were your thing?"

"Yeah, my thing, not yours."

"Well, I'll have you know the ladies think I look pretty cool in my hat,"

"Don't go there Q," I said half-jokingly. "You haven't made it to home base yet."

"My bad, my bad" Q said as he threw his hands up in surrender. "Something smells awfully good in here," he said as he walked up to me and pressed his nose up against mines while wrapping me in a soft embrace.

"Does it now?"

"Yes," he said and then planted a soft kiss on my lips.

"I'm glad you're here in a good mood, but" I said as I gently removed his hands from my waist. "Let's not forget the reason you're here. I want us to have this conversation so we can put whatever is in your head to rest. So is it something I should stomach before or after we eat."

Q walked over to the dining room, "I say after. I mean it's not that heavy, but I wouldn't want either one of us to lose our appetites with a delicious meal like this waiting on us."

"Agreed," I smiled and headed to meet Q where he stood. "Go wash your hands and we can eat."

Q and I had a wonderful dinner conversation, laughing and reminiscing on the good times we shared.

"Yeah, it wasn't all bad," Q said as he gave me a sexy stare.

"No, it wasn't."

"So do you think thing will ever be right with us again?"

"Is this the conversation that you want to have?"

"Yes, and no," Q said as he got up from his chair that was sitting across from me and came to sit right next to me. He turned my chair and had us facing one another. "It's so much to say, I don't know where to start."

"Just start."

"Tiffany may be pregnant."

"She told me."

"She told you?"

"Yeah, she came by not too long ago and dropped her bomb off. I didn't let it affect me because I know that we were both out there doing dirt so there are some consequences that we must face because of it."

"Alyssa, I know how this is going to sound, but I promise you, I would never start rebuilding our relationship on lies. I have never slept with another woman and that includes Tiffany."

"What!" I screamed in disbelief as I got up from my chair. I didn't know what to think, his words sounded so sincere but near impossible. There was also the fact that if what he was saying was true then I was the only one in this marriage who had crossed the ultimate line. I didn't want to face that truth. Q got up from his seat and faced me and then he placed my hands into his.

"I know it sounds crazy, but baby, I never did more than kiss her and the last time I checked kissing don't make no babies."

"This is a lot to swallow, Q."

"Why do you think I was so upset when I saw you at Ahmad's place? I knew what you were about to do in there and I can guarantee you it was a lot more than I've done. That's why I was angry, and that's why I smacked you." Q dropped my hands as if the visual of that memory was still fresh in his mind. He turned away from me and just stood there.

I admit it was a bit dramatic even for me, but it helped me to believe his words. I could feel his pain and my heart hurt that I couldn't offer him the same truth. I walked up and touched him on his back. He didn't object, so I moved my body closer to his, I wrapped my arms around his waist and laid my head on his back.

At first he just stood there void of any emotion. Then he took my arms into his. We stayed this way allowing our hearts to reconnect to one another. It was time standing still just for us to wake up and realize what we were really losing.

"I'm so sorry," Q said.

"So am I baby," I said as I held him tighter, "so am I."

When Q turned to face me there were tears in his eyes. "Are you still with him?"

"I never was, well not the way you think. We slept together once. I know the number doesn't matter, but…" I didn't know what could come after but to make this any easier for him, for me.

"When?"

"Q," I said praying he didn't want to really know the truth in that. My heart raced as my mind contemplated whether or not I would lie to Q. I wondered if I ever had, and couldn't for the life of me remember a time when I did.

"When, Alyssa?"

"The last time we were together."

"We, meaning you and I?"

"Yes."

Q backed up and bit his lip. I could tell that he wanted to hit something or someone but he did neither.

"What's funny is that I knew it, the day you came running up the stairs, all of a sudden wanting to please me orally, I knew then. What sealed it for me is when I smelled him on you, Alyssa." Q said matter of factly as the tears that he was holding back now made their way down his face as did mine.

"I showered, Q."

"That doesn't matter, Alyssa. A man can smell another man on his woman, I don't care how many showers you take." Q said as he visibly struggled with keeping his tone tolerable. "You didn't think after 8 years of marriage that I couldn't feel the difference?" he asked as he tilted his head to the side.

I knew that Q's questions were rhetorical, and even if they weren't they were not questions that I could answer. As much as I didn't want to, I said three words that I hoped would make things better.

"I'm so sorry,"

"I know you are."

"So where do we go from here?"

"We keep going in the same direction we're heading. We really do have a long road ahead of us, but I think you're worth it. I know I am."

"You are," I said as I wiped the tears from my eyes, then wiped my hands on my pants. "So, what about Tiffany?" Although it may have seemed as if I was trying to shift the conversation, I wasn't. I needed to know where our relationship was really heading.

"I ended that relationship before I began anew with you. I didn't want us to start off on the wrong foot."

"And the baby?"

"I don't even know if she's pregnant or not, but I do know the baby isn't mine if she is."

"How can you be so sure?"

"You really haven't been listening have you? I....have.... not......slept....with.....anyone....but....you!" Q said emphasizing every word as if that would allow me to hear his words clearly.

"Baby, listen to me" I said as I sat back down at the table. "I understand the words; that is not what I am having trouble with. I am however finding it difficult to believe that you guys have been living together for over a year and not once did you slip inside her.

I'm not trying to flip any scripts or anything; I just want what's true." I walked back over to my chair and sat down.

"And that's what I'm giving you," Q said as he sat back in his chair facing me once again. He took my hands into his. "There is no reason for me to lie to you, not right now, not about this. A baby can't be swept under the rug. Now, I more than anyone know how crazy this sounds, but I also know what I wanted in that relationship and this one. I had no intention of sleeping with her until she and I were married and I kept true to that. I also kept true to my vows to you."

"Not really, Q" I said as I pulled my hands from his. "Even if what you're saying is true, breaking vows comes in many forms and the fact that she was even in your life says you broke our vows."

"Listen," Q said as he slid to the edge of his chair and pulled me closer to him. "I understand that, but I also understand that I don't want to argue any more tonight. I just want to enjoy being with you," he said as he kissed my lips softly, gently then passionately. That was all that it took for Q to get us going in the right direction again.

I Woke Up....

the next morning, feeling better than I had in a while. I stretched long and wide, as my smile mirrored my action. Q is such a wonderful man, and right now, all I could do was thank God that we were on our way to a happy second chance. The sun kissed my eyelids softly and I smiled wider. I had such a beautiful night with Q that I had forgotten to close my blinds.

We sat up talking and laughing the night away like teenagers falling in love all over again. I hated when he left, but I agreed with him that it was best. I rolled over, ready to start the day when I felt my cell phone still resting beneath the pillow from the day before. I had completely forgotten about it.

Looking at the screen I saw that I 16 notifications. I touched the screen and let it display my missed calls and text. 3 were from Tee, 1 was my mother, 2 from Q and the rest were Ahmad. I didn't know why he was suddenly sweating me, and I wasn't even sure that it mattered. Things were looking good for me and Q. More importantly, I was happy. I didn't have time to let my mind rest on thoughts of Ahmad. I turned the volume back up and put the phone down on the nightstand.

I got out the bed and went to the bathroom to start my morning activities. Right after brushing my teeth and washing my face, I heard my phone going off. I walked back into the room and looked at the clock, it was just shy of 8:00 a.m. I picked the phone up hoping that it wasn't Ahmad. I smiled as Q's picture flashed on the screen.

"Hey you," I said as I sat back down on the bed.

"Good morning. Did you sleep well?"

"I did. How about you?"

"I never sleep well when I'm not with you, but I slept."

"Aaaaaagggggghhhhh!!!!!!" I said giving Q the impression that I was throwing up. "After a night like we had, you're calling with some tired lies."

"Hey, I'm offended, what makes you think I'm lying?"

"Hmmmm, we can start with the fact that you have your own apartment outside of our home and have had it for how long?"

"That's just so I can get some peaceful sleep. That is not the same thing as sleeping well."

"Yeah, okay. Leave it to you to try to play on words. So what do I owe this call to, so early? How did you know I wouldn't be sleeping in?"

"I didn't. I was hoping I was waking you up. You know how you do; you love to sleep in, especially since you're your own boss now."

"You don't know me," I said smiling wide, because he actually knew me pretty well. It is rare that I am out of the bed before 9 lately.

"Are you interested in breakfast? IHOP? Justins?"

"Now, you know I'm not passing on that offer. What time?"

"How about an hour?"

"You're on," I said smiling as I pressed end and raced toward the closet. Q always teased me about how long it took for me to get ready. I thought I was pretty good, but he swears I take hours. I would show him. I was going to be looking my best in record time.

I heard my phone going off again and debated on answering it. It was just like Q to try and steal some of my time. It stopped ringing and immediately started ringing again. I jogged back in there quickly, pressed talk without looking at the screen.

"This better be good," I said huffing lightly. I really needed to get back into the gym. This was ridiculous.

"Alyssa."

I pulled the phone from my ear and looked at the screen. I knew his voice but wanted the confirmation anyways. Ahmad's picture was on the screen.

"Yes," I said curtly.

"It's Ahmad."

"I know."

"Did you get my messages?"

"I haven't had the time to check them. What's going on?"

"Can we meet somewhere and talk?"

"Doubt it."

"Alyssa, no matter when or what time, or what we were going through, I have never denied you my time. If you ever needed to talk I was there for you. Now you're telling me you can't return the favor?"

I hated that I couldn't refute his claim. "When?" I asked in surrender.

"I don't know. Can we meet sometime today?"

I thought about the plans I had with Q and didn't know how long they would be. "Tomorrow's better."

"Then, tomorrow it is. Would you like to stop by here or do you want to meet at the Waffle House?"

"The Waffle House is fine," I said quick and abrupt. Now that I knew Q's apartment was next to his I was not going to chance meeting him awkwardly again. Besides, as much as I wanted to hate Ahmad for the way he had been treating me, I didn't and therefore, I didn't trust myself alone with him either.

I hung up with the feeling that I had just put the car in reverse on my relationship with Q.

So What Are...

we going to do?" She asked oblivious to the cold stare he showered on her.

"Why are you asking me what are we going to do? I don't plan on doing anything. Who's to say the baby is even mine."

"I say. You're the only one I've slept with in years, so please don't go there."

"Not according to the meeting we had. Did you forget about that? You had two lovers in the same room and now you're back at my door telling me something I refuse to believe."

"I'm telling you the truth," she said as she went and sat in the chair. He didn't want to let her in his apartment again. He wanted her to be clear and understand that their relationship was over.

He wasn't sure what game she was playing with this sudden pregnancy but he really didn't want to be a part of it. He felt that he should try a softer approach.

"Listen, Tiffany. You are a very beautiful woman by any man's standard. Before all of this chaos, I would really have loved to be your man, but too much has happened and I don't have no love for drama."

"I'm not asking to be your woman, and I don't want you to be my man. I want you to be a father to our child, nothing more, nothing less."

"I'll be a father when the blood test confirms it not your word. Until then, I think we've said all that needs to be said."

She stood to leave, anger in her eyes, but nothing she said or did could penetrate him now. He knew she was a bad move when he met her. She brushed past him, but her small weight did nothing to move him. He opened the door, she stormed out. He hoped it would be for the last time, but everything was telling him that it wasn't.

He sat down on the chair and laid his head back. He was tired. He needed to do everything he could to get his life in some type of working order. It was beyond chaotic. His visit to the doctor, Tiffany, nothing seemed to fit any more.

Everything always seemed right when Alyssa was around. He smiled more, he laughed more. The regrets he had with her were building and he knew if nothing else, his life wasn't going to be happy unless she was in it.

MY PLATE WAS....

half-eaten. I made sure to arrive before Ahmad, order and eat before he showed his face. I didn't know what he needed to talk about, but since Q hadn't fessed up to being the origin, it must be Ahmad who will. Whatever the conversation contained, I knew it would quickly cause me to lose my appetite.

When Ahmad walked in, he was as sexy as ever. I told my mind to stop playing the games that my heart didn't want to participate in. I focused my thoughts on Q. When he reached the table he smiled, my heart thumped. The Issey Miyake tantalized my senses, another beat. I closed my eyes and said a prayer. This man was my kryptonite. He affected me in ways that Q did not. I love Q, he is my comfort, my security, my happiness, my love but Ahmad, Ahmad is my passion, my stimulant.

I pushed the sausage and eggs around the plate with my fork, trying to give myself a moment to regain control of my being before I looked back up at Ahmad.

"So, I see you started without me," he said. The sound of his voice sent shivers down my spine. A tear escaped my eye, because

I was angry that I still wasn't over this man, even though I wanted to be.

"I didn't get the impression that you came here to eat," I said.

"So, what are the tears for?" he asked as he nodded his head toward me.

"Tear," I corrected as I wiped the lone tear from my face.

"Okay, I'll stand corrected. Doesn't look like you have fresh onions on your plate so, what's going on?"

"Nothing you need to concern yourself with. What did you want to talk about?" I asked as I let my fork fall to the plate.

"Alyssa," he said as he reached for my hands that I quickly placed in my lap and sat straight up. "Okay, I understand your position. I'll cut to the chase. I know that we haven't been talking much lately. I've been on the injured reserve," he said as he laughed and waved his bandaged hand.

It was the first time since he arrived that I noticed his hand was wrapped with white bandages. The meeting, the gun shot, all flashed quickly through my mind.

"So, how is it?"

"Healing slowly."

Before my mind could stop me, I had reached out and gently touched his wounded hand. He stared me in the eye.

"That made it feel better."

"Whatever," I said as I looked away from his gaze and placed my hand back in my lap. "You know that Q wasn't trying to hurt you?"

"I'm not so sure about that," he said as he leaned back in his seat.

"If he wanted to hurt you he would have."

"Uh, he did," he said as he waved his hand again for emphasis.

"You know what I mean. The price would have been a lot heftier than that. And what's more, he would have been justified."

"How so?"

"You were in his home, with a gun, threatening the life of his family."

"I was an invited guest whose life was threatened."

"You slept with his wife."

"His wife slept with me, willingly, lovingly."

"Okay, this isn't where I want this conversation to go."

"But it is where I want it. Alyssa, I know you like being in control, but sometimes it's not your option to be. You have a real hard time letting the man take the lead. That's why we keep butting heads."

"No, we keep butting heads because you keep dogging me."

"You don't really believe that do you?"

"Actually, I do."

Ahmad looked surprised, then he swept his face with his good hand, he shook his head.

"How did we get here, Alyssa?"

"Your guess is as good as mine."

"This is why they say you should never ruin a good friendship for an attraction."

Now I was getting mad, and I was glad, it was taking my mind off of all the lustful thoughts I had been having of him since he sat down.

"First of all, Ahmad, we were never friends," I said as my head involuntarily did the Black girl roll. "Secondly, the attraction wasn't mutual," I said as the pain of those words settled into my heart giving me better bearing. "Now I will admit to having an attraction to you that I let get way too out of control, but I'm trying to correct that and you just keep showing up."

183

"Maybe because the attraction is mutual," he said and my heart skipped a beat. "Did you ever think about that? Or maybe, just maybe, it's more than an attraction, Alyssa," another skip. "Maybe, I love you," my heart stopped.

I couldn't breathe, I had no words, I fell back in my seat and let the words hit me, and they did, hard. I wanted to run, but I couldn't move.

"Call me when your divorce is final," Ahmad said as he stood and walked out as smoothly as he entered. I watched him walk to his car, get in and pull off, then I breathed, and then I cried.

Please Pick Up Tee....

I shouted into the receiver as the phone rang. Twenty minutes would pass before the waitress would pull me out of my distressed state asking if I was done. I nodded my head, placed a twenty dollar bill on the table and slowly left the restaurant.

I had to talk to Tee; she would make some sense of this game that the devil was playing with me. She was my rock. Wisdom poured from her like God had blessed her to be my sanity in an insane world.

She didn't answer. I hung up the line and dialed her right back.

"What the hell is so important?" she asked as she picked up this time.

"Tee," I half sang "I need my big sister right now. You would think the older I get the less dependent I would be on you, but uh, no. My problems just change."

"What's going on, Alyssa."

"You know Q and I are really putting an effort to getting our marriage back on track, right?"

"Old news, fast forward."

"I just met with Ahmad."

"Now that's some juice, for what? You wanted him to tap.... that..... ass," she said laughing at her own joke. I didn't join her.

"He said he loves me."

"Woooo, now that's some shit right there. Do I need to go pop some popcorn?"

"Tee, I need you to be serious right now."

"Whoa, back up. You rang my line for my help. You don't get to dictate how I say what I say. Okay!"

I felt like a kid being reprimanded. Tee would never let us put her in check, whether she was wrong or right didn't matter, which is why Bree and I rarely even tried.

"So what do you think?"

"What am I supposed to think?"

"I mean, you were all on Ahmad's bandwagon, saying how he's such a good guy and everything."

"And he is, but so is Q. I love my brother-in-law. Alyssa, how do you get yourself into these messes."

"Let me see, I think it was the letter in the mail that told me which direction to go to get into the best mess possible."

"Oh, so now you got jokes," Tee said, but neither one of us laughed.

"No, I don't. I've got problems that need solutions."

"Did you ever figure out who has herpes?"

"No, and no one seems to be fessing up to it either."

"Well, maybe it's neither one of them. They did say there was no way to tell its origin, so maybe you got it in high school or something. I mean, you aren't Jezebel, but you're no saint either."

"Hey pot, I'm kettle, nice to meet you."

"Alyssa, I'm just saying. Just like you're getting angry at me right now, you could be getting mad at the wrong person in that situation too."

"I'm not mad at anyone," I said before I realized that it was a lie, "well I guess I am a little, but only because I don't care what anyone says, this thing really does sit in the lap of Q, Ahmad, or Tiffany."

"Or you. Pushing past that, if you were to determine the exact origin to be Q or Ahmad, then what? Will that help you make the decision you have right now?"

"Yes."

"How?"

"I don't want to be with anyone who passed something that I can never get rid of to me."

"So then stop seeing them both."

"What?"

"You heard me, if the possibility is that one or both passed it, then just do yourself a favor and cut them both loose now."

"So forget about the fact that I love them, I mean him."

"No you meant them, but if you're not making love a factor when you find out the results, then it doesn't need to be a factor now. Move on with your life, Alyssa. Stop feeding on bullshit."

"Yeah, alright Tee," I said as I ended the call, started the ignition and turned the radio on to make my way home. God has a funny way of speaking, I thought as I listened to Stevie Wonder's *All in Love is Fair* float through my stereo. I turned the volume up and let the lyrics saturate. I wondered how much truth they held, as the words cut into my heart sharper than a two-edge sword.

The pain was almost unbearable. I never thought I would be that woman, torn between two men, loving them both.

A writer takes his pen
To write the words again
That all in love is fair

In All Your...

getting, get an understanding. This was something that I would have to work out on my own. Every time I wanted to think on the matters of the heart, I found myself in a dark room letting music counsel me. It was a habit that I was sure I inherited from my mother.

I booted up the laptop, turned on Pandora and selected the Minnie Riperton station. I listened as she bellowed out her classic, *Lovin' You* and let thoughts of Q and Ahmad play in my head. Song after song played, from Sade, Jill Scott, Stevie Wonder and once it was all said and done, I was no more the wiser.

My cell vibrated, Q's face flashed on the screen. I didn't want to talk, but it wasn't fair to him. I answered.

"Hello,"

"Wow, is everything okay."

"Yeah, just doing a lot of thinking," I said as I tried to shake the sadness from my voice.

"Sounds like more than thinking, going on. Sounds like you're going through a decision making process."

"How so?"

"I hear the music in the background, Lyss. Your voice is solemn. I know you better than you think. Eight years may not be much to some, but if it's used wisely, you can gain a lot of knowledge about somebody. Especially if you're interested."

I was crouched on the floor of the sitting area, with my head against the wall. I looked up into nothing, because it was too dark to see anything, but I know God knew He was my target. I said a silent prayer.

"Alyssa, are you still with me?"

"I am,"

"Do you want me to come over?"

"Not tonight."

"So tomorrow?"

"Yeah, maybe. I'll call you, okay?"

"Yeah, okay," he said before disconnecting our line.

Q called right back, I hit talk but didn't have more pep in my voice than I had a few moments ago.

"He's back isn't he?" Q asked catching me completely off guard.

"What?"

"Alyssa, we have been doing so well remaining honest in our new beginnings, please don't change that now."

"Ahmad called yesterday wanting to meet. I said no at first, but he reminded me of how many times I was on the other end of that same question, so I gave in. I didn't know how I would feel when I saw him again, but when he got there," I stopped. I had given Q more than I wanted, but I respected the fact that he wanted us to be honest.

"When he got there, what?"

"Everything I have ever felt for him resurfaced."

"So what does that mean for us?"

"I don't know, he told me he loves me."

"And you believe him."

"I don't know what to believe right now, Q."

"Do you believe me?"

"I want to, but so much doesn't add up with you. I need everything to add up, to make sense."

"You're not looking for what makes sense, you're looking for perfection and right now, it looks like you're looking for a way out. I want to be the motive not the consequence."

"So what are you saying?"

"I'm sure I don't have to break it down for you, Alyssa. You're way too smart for that."

"Humor me, Q. I don't want there to be room for misinterpretation."

"I love you, unconditionally. I want you to be my wife, for better or for worse. I watched you fall in love with another man, all while telling me it was all in my mind and now with knowing what's true, I still want you, but I refuse to be an afterthought. If I am not who you want, then say that, but don't choose me because you can't have him. Choose me because you want and love me just as much as I do you."

"I do love you, Q. Everything isn't as simple as you want it to be. I can't put this in a neat little box and tie it with a pretty red bow and make everything alright again. So much has transpired between us on both of our ends, not just mine. Just as much as you have put up with craziness, so have I. You're not alone in this, you never have been, but so many times I feel like I am."

"You won't let me in. As hard as I try, I can't seem to break this tough exterior you have up to shield away any chance at real love."

"Q, I don't want to talk about this anymore."

"Let me come see you, Alyssa." Q said, his words sounding passionate, desperate.

"Okay," I said, once again surrendering to a man's request that didn't meet my desire. I was beginning to understand why my life was so chaotic. "Wait, Q. Not tonight, let me have tonight. We'll talk tomorrow."

"Okay, tomorrow."

I turned the phone off. Went back to the laptop, placed the cursor on the button, 'I'm still listening' and let Pandora continue to counsel me.

Q'S FLOWERS ARRIVED....

as beautiful as they were last week. I took last weeks and placed them in the kitchen, and left the fresh roses on the console in the foyer. He was really working overtime and I was enjoying the moment. Although, I couldn't help but wonder how long the moment would last. I decided to stop harping on the particulars and just enjoy Q, enjoy life. I picked up my cell and called him.

"Thank you, they're beautiful," I said once Q picked up the phone.

"What is?" he asked sounding as if I had just awaken him from a sound sleep.

"The flowers."

"You wait a whole week to thank me for flowers?"

Thank God I was quick on my feet, because it became very apparent that the fresh flowers were not from Q.

"Late is always better than never," I said in a tone I thought was convincing.

"Let me guess, Ahmad sent you flowers today, huh?" Apparently, Q was quick on his feet as well.

"I can't say for sure, I thought they were from you."

"So you was just gone let me believe you were talking about last week's flowers?"

"Didn't see a need for you to think otherwise," I said as I walked back to the foyer and pulled the card from the flowers.

No longer wanting to hide behind maybe, I love you, Alyssa, more than words can say – Ahmad.

"And so?"

"And so, what?"

"Either you keep trying to play me for a fool, or you really don't understand the extent to which I know you, Alyssa. You've read the card now, and I'm correct, right? Ahmad is stepping up his game."

"Yes."

"I'm not worried, you know."

"I never wanted you to be."

"Good. What time am I picking you up?"

"When did we decide that we were going somewhere today?"

"Just now."

I looked at the clock, it was 9:15 a.m. "Will this be a morning, afternoon or evening date?"

"Why not all day?"

"My, my, aren't we greedy."

"Call it whatever you want, lady. So, what time?"

"How about 12:00?"

"Works for me, see you then."

A smile crossed my face at the thought of spending an entire day with Q.

Six Kids Were....

the evidence to his love of children. He loved them equally, he loved them genuinely. Last year, he would have been pleased to bring home his seventh child, but Indya refused him this opportunity, choosing to abort his seed before they even had the chance to breathe. His heart hurt for his unborn child and if there was anything that he could have done to prevent the tragedy from taking place he would have.

He looked at Indya different from that day forth which made their relationship end quickly thereafter. He could no longer stand to look her in the face. He wondered what it was in her that reminded him of Alyssa, and for the life of him he couldn't figure it out because she was as far from Alyssa as east was from west. In fact, she couldn't hold a candle to Alyssa's shadow.

It wasn't that she wasn't beautiful, she was. It was the fact that her beauty was only reflected in her outer appearance. It had no depth, no weight and for that he lost interest in her. Still, he thought he could make things work and they could be happy, if only she had kept his child.

Now, not quite a year later he found himself in an equally devastating situation. He had no more love for Tiffany than he had for Indya and now she was claiming to be bearing his seed. For a man who strapped up like he did, he was coming up with the short end of the stick. He went through his condoms checking them for damages or possible tampering.

He couldn't find anything and yet there was still the possibility that once again he could be welcoming in his seventh child. As much as he loved kids, he prayed that Tiffany's claim would prove false. He could have dealt with Indya, but Tiffany was another story altogether. Besides, if he had half a chance with Alyssa, he couldn't have Tiffany as a constant in his life.

My Cell Phone ....

rang just as I turned the corner. "What, you have ESP or something?" I asked with all seriousness in my tone.

"Why do you say that?"

"I'm headed to your house as we speak."

"And what makes you think I'm home," Ahmad said.

"I don't know if you're there or not, but I needed to return something, so if you weren't there, I was planning to leave it on your doorstep."

"You didn't like the flowers."

"Why do you and Q seem to think y'all know me better than I know myself?"

"I don't know about Quan, but I do know you. Now whether or not it's better than you know yourself is for you to decide. I tend to look past the words you kick out. I prefer to look into their meaning, thereby giving me a very clear view of who you are. So yes, I do know you."

"Uh huh, all that and more, are you home or not?" I asked, opting not to challenge his statement right now.

"I'm here. Have you eaten?"

"This is not a social call, Ahmad."

"But it can be."

Against my better judgment, I agreed to have lunch with Ahmad. Q and I had a wonderful date yesterday and more and more, I was beginning to believe that he is who God meant for me to be with. I needed to put this thing with Ahmad to bed. I knocked on his door and he opened within seconds.

Again, Ahmad had come to the door with no shirt on, but this time he didn't have on pajama pants either. He had a towel wrapped around his waist, water dripping from his body and I swear the beads were forming the word sexy. My body was reacting faster than my brain could think.

"Uh, ummm, I thought you wanted to have lunch," I said clutching the vase of beautiful flowers close, praying for strength.

"I do," he replied coyly. "I just got out of the shower, do you want to come in for a moment, while I get dressed. I won't be long. I promise."

His eyes were beckoning me to come in to do more than wait. My mind had caught up with my body and told me to run. I agreed. "No," I said firmly. I handed him the vase, as he reached for them the towel dropped and I was so disappointed that I would not be able to take advantage of such a beautiful creation.

"I'll wait for you in the car," I said as I turned and ran back down the stairs as fast as my feet could carry me. I jumped in the car like someone was chasing me. I crossed my legs and squeezed tight. I placed my head on the steering wheel. "Lord, if I never needed you before, I need you right now."

After a few minutes I heard a knock on my window. I panicked before looking up as I remembered this was also Q's apartment. I rolled the window down, relieved that Ahmad did not keep me waiting long.

"Are you okay?" he asked.

"Yeah, I'm fine. So, where to?"

"Do you want me to drive?"

"No, we can just take separate cars. I'll follow you."

"That doesn't technically make it a date."

"Ahmad!"

"I'm just saying," he said as he threw his hands up in surrender and walked toward his car. I bit my lip and started my car up. Nothing is ever easy when you want it to be. I followed Ahmad to Gladys Knights Chicken and Waffles. It was one of my favorite spots and I wondered if I had ever confessed that to him.

Ahmad was out of the car and at my door before I could even turn my ignition off. I unlocked the door and he opened it for me.

"I was coming," I said as I took the hand he held out for me.

"I know this. You must not be used to a gentleman, huh."

"Oh, you got jokes already, I see."

Ahmad held my hand as we walked to the door. A pretty young lady walked out as we entered.

"Anthony?" she said as she looked at Ahmad.

"Excuse me?" he asked looking caught off guard.

"Anthony Thomas, right?" she asked again.

"I'm sorry, you must be mistaken. That's not my name."

"Of course it's not," she said as she nodded her head, smiled and then continued out the door.

It was a very strange transaction. People mistook people for someone else all the time. I have had it happen to me once or twice, but this seemed different. The lady seemed quite sure that she wasn't mistaken. Ahmad wasn't my man so I didn't see any need for him to lie to me or her. I shrugged it off and went in to enjoy my lunch.

"So, old girlfriend?" I asked Ahmad as we took our seats.

"Now you know if it was an old girlfriend, she would definitely know my name."

"True, but she definitely seemed to know you from somewhere. You do have the look that is hard to forget."

"Thank you," he responded to my compliment but left my inquiry where it stood. I backed off, it really wasn't that important.

The waitress came and took our order. I already knew that I wanted the shrimp omelet, and Ahmad wound up with the Midnight Train. We chatted lightly while we waited for our order. I didn't want to take the conversation where it needed to go until I finished my omelet. I didn't need anything standing in the way of me finishing every bite of that.

Ahmad paid the bill, I was glad, because that was another thing that I wasn't trying to get stuck with. I mean, Ahmad never struck me to be that guy, but who knows what guy he is, when things don't work according to his plans.

"So," I said as we exited the restaurant, "I wanted to talk about this 'confession' that you dropped in my lap last week."

"Alyssa, you're a trip. I didn't make any confessions. I'm just tired of denying what I really feel about you."

I leaned up against my car. "And so you think its love?"

"I don't make it a habit of saying what I think and just stick to verbalizing what I know. It cuts down on confusion."

"Why now?"

"Alyssa, it's been two years. You wearing a brother down," he said as he laughed, I didn't see the humor. "Lighten up," he said as he touched my chin lightly. "You don't have to be so serious all the time. Life is for loving and living."

Ahmad stepped closer to me. I put my hand on his chest, stopping him from coming too close.

"Alyssa," he said softly as he gently held the hand that I had placed against his chest. He kissed it softly and I pulled my hand away. "Why are you fighting me now? You have been chasing us, this for two years now. So, why are you avoiding the inevitable?"

"I think you and I have two different versions of what's inevitable. My version ends with Q and I rekindling a love once lost."

Ahmad stepped back. "Q? What happened to getting a divorce?"

"We have decided to forego the divorce. I love him, Ahmad." I admitted, however, I couldn't look him in the eye when I said it. I turned and looked back toward the restaurant.

"We," he said with a wicked grin on his face. "So, Quan is in on this decision, and he knows this?"

"Look," I said as my anger began to rise. "I know that you think I make it a habit of chasing men, but I don't. I didn't chase you; that's just what your ego wants to believe."

"My heart wants to believe that you love me with the same fire and passion that you did the night we made love."

"Oh so now we made love, it was just sex remember?"

Ahmad walked up to me and pressed his body against mine. Everything in me wanted to push him away. Well almost everything, my body wanted him to stay. My body won. He bent down and kissed me softly on the lips, my mind was losing the battle. Everything that I knew was wrong, now felt right. My knees felt weak. The passion in his touch intensified as his kiss became more urgent.

I heard the sound of people walking, and talking. I wanted so desperately to break his embrace. My arms betrayed my desire as they wrapped around his body and pulled him in closer. When our lips parted, I was spent. He could have asked me to walk to the moon with him and I would have.

Ahmad cupped my face in his hands and pressed his forehead against mine. "We are not meant for next lifetime, Alyssa. We are meant for this one." He said as the heat from his breath warmed my face. He pulled away from the embrace that I had comforted myself in.

"Call me when your divorce is final," he said as he walked away, leaving me standing against my car, breathless, wanting him, wanting us.

He Watched As....

Alyssa came up the steps to visit another man. He wouldn't let her know that he saw her. He saw the flowers in her hand and knew that she had a purpose, a plan and he would let her see it to its end. They had spent the day together, yesterday, talking about everything and he knew in his heart that she was the one he was supposed to spend the rest of his life with. He meant his vows then and he meant them even more now.

He wished that his window allowed him a view of Gary's front door, but it didn't. He was glad to see Alyssa running down the stairs shortly after she arrived. He was glad, until a few minutes later he heard Gary leaving too. He cracked his door open and saw that Alyssa was still there waiting for him. He wondered where they were headed and contemplated following them, but then. He felt her hand on his back.

"What has you so occupied that you're not spending any time with me?"

He shut his door and turned toward Tiffany.

He Pulled from...

the lot feeling more emotions than he was ever used to feeling. He prided himself on being an Alpha male and with that he didn't allow himself to delve too deeply into emotions. Alyssa was tearing him apart. No woman has ever made him feel the way she does. When she hurts he hurt. He had tried to keep her at bay, and for two years he had succeeded. He wasn't sure what changed or even how but he was determined to make her the next Mrs. Gary Ahmad.

It sickened him to know that Quan was trying to work things out with Alyssa when he knew first hand that he was still dealing with Tiffany. He was no saint, he had his own cross to bear as well, but he would never step to another woman if he had half a chance with Alyssa. She deserved so much more than he or Quan had ever offered her, and he for one would make it right. Quan on the other hand was still trying to run game.

He had told him before that real men don't play games, but he could tell that Quan was one of those dudes that you had to show better than you could tell them and he was just the man to do it. He owed him for the constant sucker punches he would get in on him. He let him keep the first one, but as Ahmad stared at his wounded hand, he knew he wasn't going to give Quan another opportunity of having the upper hand.

As he pulled into his spot he smirked as he watched Quan and Tiffany talking outside the apartment. From where he stood it looked more like they were arguing, but he knew if he waited he could catch them in a compromising position. He got out the car and leaned against the hood of his car. He quickly programmed the camera on his phone to stamp the date and time.

He waited patiently as he tried to listen to what they were discussing. He couldn't make out their words and he didn't care enough to find out. After a few moments the argument subsided and Tiffany started laughing, he watched a small smile form on Quan's face as well. He snapped the shot and waited. Quan placed his hand on the small of Tiffany's back and walked her down the stairs, Ahmad snapped another shot.

That was enough for him. He went into his gallery, clicked the two recent shots and sent them to Alyssa. He typed in the comment:

Is this really who you want to give your heart to?

Ahmad placed the phone in his pocket and crossed his arms. He stared at Quan hard, hoping he'd open the door for him to go in on him. Quan stared back at him, seemingly unfazed by the mean mug he was giving him. Tiffany smiled and nodded her head in acknowledgement. He nodded his head back.

Once Quan had gotten Tiffany safely in her car and on her way, he headed back to his apartment. He stopped in front of Ahmad. Ahmad stood.

"Is there something you want to say, my man?" Ahmad asked.

"You're not even worth my time," Q said as he started to walk away.

"I never wanted to be, now Alyssa is another story," Ahmad said hoping he had struck a nerve.

Q turned back toward Ahmad, "Alyssa and I are one in the same. You deal with her, you deal with me."

"From where I'm standing, looks like you got your hands full with Tiffany. So I'll help you out. I'll take Alyssa off your hands, because you and I both know she deserves a lot better than what you're giving her."

Q stepped toward Ahmad with his fist balled, then suddenly without warning, he stepped back and started laughing hysterically. He laughed so hard you would have thought Kevin Hart was there giving a live performance.

Ahmad stood wondering where he was going with this. He didn't see a damn thing funny. He raised his eyebrow wondering if Quan was crazy. He let his hand rest on his 38. He didn't know what the hell was going on with Quan, but after dealing with him in the past, he wasn't taking any chances now.

Q stopped laughing and his face was now void of emotion. He stared Ahmad in the eye and said, "You know what, maybe you need to go find some kids to play with, because I'm a grown ass man, I don't have time for your games," and with that he walked off and into his apartment.

Ahmad's cell phone vibrated. Alyssa had responded back to his picture mail:

WTH?

THE PICTURES ANGERED....

me and not for their content either. I was pissed that Ahmad would send me this trash. I text him back. He called.

"Hello," I answered not bothering to hide my discontent.

"I know you're mad Alyssa, but I thought you should know. I mean you're at lunch talking about how you guys decided to work on your marriage and it seems to me like you're the only one working on it."

"Ahmad, that's not for you to decide. For you to take it upon yourself and send me something crazy like this shows me you're not the mature man that I thought you were."

"Wait, hold up. Are you trying to check me?"

"I'm stating facts, Ahmad."

"Alyssa, I'm trying to stay cool because I really want a future with you, but you're pushing it real hard right now."

"How so?"

"When old dude went upside your head that day you was pissed at me for not telling you before what I already knew, now that I'm not only telling you, I'm showing you, you want to come at me with some bullshit. I got mad love for you, but I knew from the day I saw you that you was gone be a handful. That's one of the reasons why I keep trying to leave you alone."

I took a breath. Ahmad was right in more ways than one. I didn't want to admit it, but true to form my anger was being misplaced. I didn't expect to receive picture mail from Ahmad as if I hired him to do my dirty work for me, but if I would have found out that he knew again and didn't say anything, I would have hit the roof. I bit my lip trying to figure out a way to balance this out.

"I'm sorry," I said, it seemed the best place to start.

"It's cool, Alyssa. Why do you love dealing in drama?"

"I don't, it follows me."

"Nothing or no one can do more than you allow. Alyssa, I know you want things to work between you and Quan, but I want what's best for you. Sometimes you have to let go of your past to take hold of your future. You are going to continue being confused if you keep trying to hold on to both."

"That advice would be so much easier to swallow if it wasn't coming from someone with their own ulterior motive."

"Swallow your ego first, Alyssa. See this is why you can't reveal too much to a woman like you, you're not ready to handle truth. If I tell you I love you, don't get cocky, because there's another woman just as beautiful and smart as you around the corner. My advice is not coming from an ulterior motive, it's coming from wisdom. I'm not telling you to leave Quan, and I'm not saying come be with me. I am saying make your decision wisely and stop basing it on past hang ups."

"I hear you."

"Good, now hear this, because it's the last time I'll say it. Should you decide to sign them papers, call me."

Ahmad hung up. I bit my lip and thought over his words. He really did have a way with them.

IT WAS OUR....

last session before our court date with Judge Michaels. I had
so much on my mind between what I thought and what I believed.
What I wanted to do and what I needed to do. Everything was a
tug of war. I wanted to blame Q or Ahmad, but the truth is I
played with fire, and as everyone knows when you play with fire,
you risk getting burned. I got burned in more ways than one and
now I was living with the consequences.

I sat on the couch next to Q. We had been twice a month for
the past six months. With each visit I had grown more comfortable
with the setting, the couch, the counseling, but today I wasn't.
Today, I felt like I was on the outside looking in. I wanted to be
happy with Q, he makes me happy. However, I understood that I
shouldn't place my happiness in another person's care, unless that
someone was God.

"Shall we begin," Dr. Donovan asked.

"Yeah," I said as I breathed heavily and sat straight up.

"Well, that didn't sound so convincing, Alyssa. What's been
going on with you two since we last spoke?"

"Nothing much," Q said as he cleared his throat and placed his hand on mine.

"Well, nothing much if you're not factoring in the possibility that my husband may have another woman pregnant. A white woman at that," I said as I chuckled a little.

"I was wondering how many times you were going to factor in her race," Q said as he removed his hand from mine.

"Does her race matter?" Dr. Donovan asked.

"Yes and no. It matters to a degree because I feel like Black men seek out other races when they are having a hard time dealing with their own. It's a coward move."

"So now I'm a coward?" Q asked as he shifted in his seat putting space between us.

"I'm not saying you per se," I said trying to mend the fence that I was breaking apart quickly. I shifted my body to face Q, "well maybe I am. Have you ever asked yourself why you decided on Tiffany? You're fine Q, so I know you have women looking and flirting with you daily, and I'm sure more than a handful are Black. So, why did you choose her?"

"Actually, Alyssa, I didn't choose her, she chose me. I wasn't and am not looking to be with anyone but you. It wasn't my intention to begin a relationship with her. I met her after one of our arguments and she just fit. I didn't look at the color of her skin to make my determination."

"Okay, let's get off the color thing, because really that's a moot point. Let's talk about the fact that she may be carrying your child."

"I told you she's not. I don't know what I need to do for you to believe me, but I have never slept with her."

"A blood test, Q, apparently that's what it's going to take. I want to trust you but I don't want to be a fool either. You're in an almost two year relationship without any intimacy."

"I never said there wasn't intimacy. There was, there was just never penetration. I have never had sex with her, with or without a condom."

"Mr. Robertson, do you believe that it's possible for you to move forward in your marriage when there is still so much distrust in the foundation?"

"I want to because I love her, she's my world. I also know that our foundation is very weak and without a solid one, our marriage is destined to fail."

"Again," I added for emphasis.

"Mrs. Robertson, you seem to have a lot of animosity in this session. I understand your feelings toward Tiffany, but she was discussed in several sessions and I don't recall feeling this degree of emotion from you. What are your real concerns?"

I couldn't bring up the pictures Ahmad had sent for a few reasons. First, I didn't want Q to think that I had been spying on him, or worse had my lover doing it. Second, if Q knew that Ahmad had sent the pictures he would probably send him back to the hospital. I could however, open the door for him.

"I don't think he'll ever stop seeing her. I think you love her more than you do me. It was evident by the ring you gave her, Q."

"Alyssa, you don't even wear jewelry. Stop trying to find things where there is none."

"When was the last time you saw her?"

"Last week, the day after our date to be exact," Q said without hesitation. My heart smiled, I felt like I could trust him again.

"Why?"

"She came over trying to tell me that she gave me a date rape drug and that is when we conceived the baby."

My heart stopped, I took a breath.

"Did she?"

"I can't say for certain, but I seriously doubt it."

"Why is she holding on to you so tough?"

"The question should be why aren't you?"

"Q, I have been the only one fighting for this relationship for the past eight years."

"Correction, the last two years have been hell. You stopped fighting once you let Gary in the picture."

"I never stopped fighting."

"I don't believe that, Alyssa. In fact, when was the last time you've seen him?"

I didn't want to admit it, but I didn't want to lie either.

"The same day you saw Tiffany." I said and I wanted to stop there, but I could tell Q wanted to know more. "We went to lunch. I told him things were over between us. That you and I had decided to work on our marriage, but then." I stopped short of a full confession, but not short enough.

"But then what," Q said. It was obvious he was trying to keep it together. He was mad and I knew it, and what I was going to say was not going to make matters any better.

"I kissed him, not intentionally, but."

"How do you not intentionally kiss somebody, Alyssa?"

"He kissed me."

"And let me guess, you didn't stop him either. Let me go one better, you liked it? Right? Am I hitting it on the head here, Alyssa."

I didn't respond; there was no need to. He was right and there was no need denying the truth.

"Now I understand your sudden change of heart," Q said.

"That's not fair, I don't have a change of heart."

"Don't you? You're in here after all that we have been through these past weeks doubting our relationship, doubting me. As hard as I have been working to keep you in my life, you're draining me, Alyssa. Love shouldn't be this hard. I don't need the road to be easy, but it just shouldn't be this hard," Q said as he got up from the couch.

"So where are you guys going from here?" Dr. Donovan asked.

"I don't know," Q said.

"Neither do I," I replied.

Q left the office before the session ended. Dr. Donovan stared at me as if I had the answers to her unasked questions. There was time still left in our session, but like Q, I didn't want them. I smiled weakly as I got up and left the office as well.

It Would Be....

another night of me listening to Pandora laying my feelings on the line. My choice wasn't as hard as I was making it be. In fact it was rather simple. I think what was hard for me was deciding if I could walk away from a passion that was unbelievably strong. I thought about all the advice that Tee had given me on subjects like this, "that one brotha," I said aloud. Now I understood what Jayla meant.

Ahmad was just that, he was that one brotha that could put it down. Although we had only been intimate once, it was enough for me to confirm that he was my passion. Whenever he was in the room, my heart beat for him, and when he wasn't my thoughts cried out for him. My body longed for his touch.

I couldn't take away from Quan either though. He was more than just my comfort. He understood me and accepted me for who I am, with or without change. That's a whole lot more than I can say that I offer him. I feel at peace when he's home, when he's near. My heart smiles for him, and that's not factoring in how fine he is.

I looked back toward the ceiling. "Yeah, daddy, you really do have a funny sense of humor.

I was stressing, it was something I hated to do, but the court date was quickly approaching and I knew that I needed to walk in there with a concrete decision being made. I let my mind play over the time I had with each man, knowing that I would have far more happier days with Quan.

I shifted, suddenly, I was uncomfortable and I couldn't place my finger on why. I shifted again and got up from the chair. I thought about calling Tee, but decided against it because I knew that this had to be my decision, which is also why I didn't want to call Ahmad or Q. I wanted to be clear on the direction I was going in.

The discomfort stayed with me even in my standing position, I adjusted my underwear and walked to sit on the bed. I rested my head on the headboard and sighed. I no longer felt like sitting. I got up and paced the floor. The friction with each step was increasingly becoming uncomfortable. I needed to know where the issue lied. I went to the bathroom and grabbed the hand mirror. I undressed and propped my leg up on the vanity bench.

There it was the object of my discomfort staring back at me and reminding me why this decision should have never been hard. It was a single bump that most would have mistaken for a hair bump, but I knew better. I knew that I was staring back at my first outbreak. I remembered Dr. Armstrong's words and how stress could play a factor in outbreaks.

I slammed the mirror down so hard, I thought it would break, washed my hands, redressed and headed back to the room. I turned off Pandora. I didn't need to think any more. I knew what my decision should have been from the start, now it was made that much easier. I felt like a fool to have placed myself in a predicament that would allow me at forty years old to contract something I could never get rid of.

It was time for me to make wiser decisions. This was my wake up call. I was ready to listen.

I WALKED AROUND Q'S...

apartment for the first time. It was cozy and unique. I could see the effort he put into making it his. I let my hand slide across his Black Panther table as I nodded my head in approval. As nice as it was, I wondered if he would keep the apartment after we abolished the divorce papers. It felt odd being in a place that he shared with someone other than me. I didn't go into the bedroom. I didn't need to see it; in fact I didn't want to see it.

"So," I said as I walked over to the chaise and sat down. "Are you ready for tomorrow?" It was the big day that had quickly approached. The state of our marriage now rested on one day, two decisions, three people, four if you kept Tiffany in the equation, five if you counted her unborn child.

"I didn't realize it was something we needed to prepare for," Q said as he smiled and sat back in his chair.

"I love your smile."

"Is that all you love," he asked as he furrowed his eyebrows in an inquisitive stare.

"Maybe."

"Uh huh," Q said as he stood and walked toward me. He sat down on the chaise that I was occupying, our bodies were close. "Are you sure about that," he said as he leaned in closer.

"Is anyone ever sure about anything?" I asked as I stood from the chaise.

"What's going on with you, Alyssa?"

I decided not to sugarcoat it or delay the inevitable. "I'm in the midst of my first breakout," I said bluntly as I faced the door with my back toward him. I wanted to move quickly to the door and exit. I felt flush. I hated saying the words aloud. It was devastating and embarrassing.

Q walked up behind me and held me. "I'm sorry, baby."

It wasn't what I expected, yet true to form, Q always gave me what I needed. I let him hold me.

"Have you been tested yet?" I asked.

"Yes."

I turned to face him with a look of astonishment. "When were you going to tell me?"

"It didn't seem important."

"And why not?"

"Because contrary to what you want to believe, Alyssa. I'm clean. I don't have a trace of anything in my blood."

"It's not contrary to what I want to believe, Q. I'm glad you're clean. So," I said as I huffed, "when did you find out?"

"Weeks ago."

"So why are you still trying to work things out with me?"

"Is that a serious question?"

"Yes, I'm tainted, more so now, than ever before."

"Alyssa, I love you. We said for better or worse. I didn't know worse would be this bad," he said as he tilted his head to the ground and then smiled, "but I know you're worth it. I just need you to know that I am."

"I do know, Q." I said as I pounded my fist lightly on his chest. "That's where the problem is, do you realize how much easier it would be to walk away from you if you weren't such a great guy?"

"Stop trying to walk away from me."

"Okay," I said as I kissed him on the cheek. "Thanks for another wonderful day, and even better conversation."

"No need for thanks," he said as he walked me to the door. Both of our mouths dropped open as we saw Tiffany standing on the other side. I noticed that she had a slight baby bump, although it looked awkward. It made me want to go and straighten it out, like an uneven wig.

"Tiffany," I said as I tilted my head inquisitively.

"What are you doing here?" Quan said angrily still holding my arm. His grip tightened. I pulled away gently. He looked at me and said sorry, softly.

"I came to talk to you."

"About what?"

"Our baby," Tiffany said as she rubbed her baby bump.

I took notice that as she rubbed the bump it seemed to collapse. 'I see you,' I thought but I wouldn't pull her coattails in front of Q. This we would handle on our own, no drama, all peace, two grown women putting an end to this foolishness and the childish behavior that followed it.

"I'll let you two talk," I said as I looked dead at Tiffany, showing her that I was comfortable with Q. I trusted him and she was the last person I needed to worry about.

"That's not necessary," Q said as I continued to walk down the stairs.

"Sure it is, call me letter babe," I said casually while realizing that it was now her turn to hear another woman think of Q affectionately.

"You know what," Tiffany said as she lifted her shirt and pulled the manufactured pillow from her stomach. "I don't even know why I bother. You're not all that." She reached for the ring on her finger, but apparently changed her mind. "Naw, I'm keeping this for my pain and suffering she said as she followed me down the stairs.

I got in my car. 'Looks like I won't have to have that conversation after all.' I thought as I put the car in reverse and left Tiffany and her drama behind.

HE SAT IN HIS....

car seething at the sight before him. If there was ever a time he would beat a woman, this was it. He watched as Tiffany pulled a pillow away from her supposedly impregnated stomach and writhed at the lie she had told him. Everything in his mind told him that he hadn't gotten her pregnant, that there was no way in hell it was possible. Yet he believed her, he didn't understand why she would lie to him. Their relationship was over months ago.

He breathed deeply, gathered his thoughts, calmed his spirit and exited his vehicle. He shrugged his shoulders as he looked at Tiffany, she didn't seem the least bit phased at his presence.

"So, no baby after all, huh?" he asked casually. He refused to let her see the anger behind his words. She would never know that she had gotten to him.

"Oh, whatever," Tiffany said as she brushed past him as if he wasn't worthy of her time. He grabbed her arm.

"You don't have the option to walk past me without answers."

"Get your hands off of me, Ahmad. Now!"

"And if I don't," he said as he drew his face close to hers.

"This may be 2012, but not much has changed. I'm still a White woman, and you're still a Black man, so if you don't get your hands off of me, I promise you this won't be pretty."

He let her go, the truth in her words stung worse than a snake's venom. "You're right," he said as he threw his arms up in defeat. "I'm hoping that you show a little class, you know some dignity about yourself. Right now, I'm looking at you as a low-life, like trash that I shouldn't have given the time of day."

"Maybe, you shouldn't have. Do you really think your words matter to me? You are just a pawn in a bigger game, I never wanted you. Your sex was a great way to pass time, I mean you do know what you're doing there," she said with a sly grin.

"I wish I could return the compliment. I'm not about to be out here going back and forth with you. As we have both established, I'm not worth your time and you're not worth mine. So cut to the chase, answer my question and we can push on. Why did you tell me you were pregnant with my baby, when it's obvious now that you weren't pregnant at all?"

"Awww, did I hurt the poor baby's feelings?" she said as she walked closer to him. "Okay, I'll give you a cookie. The truth is this, Ahmad," she said his name as if it pained her. "You walk around like you're so hard, so macho and the reality is you're just as weak as the next man. You are so in love with Alyssa that it's killing you. Everybody can see it."

"Stop playing games, Tiffany. Get to the point."

"The point is this, sweetie. I knew if I told you that I was pregnant, you would run and tell Alyssa with the hopes that I was carrying Q's baby and that would sever their relationship for sure. So see, in the long run, I was doing us both a favor. I needed you to convince her that I was pregnant, and you did, didn't you? You

228

probably high-tailed it over their so quickly, you didn't need a vehicle to carry you," she said as she laughed in his face.

He didn't like being made a fool of, he wasn't anyone's pawn. He walked away from Tiffany before he did something that would land him in jail. She had used up all of the time he had for her.

JUDGE MICHAELS SLAMMED....

her gavel bringing court to order. Quan and I took our perspective seats. I looked over at his table and wondered what our outcome would be. I was unsure today of what I was so positive of six months ago, or six days ago for that matter. My life was on a constant shift and every time I tried to get it going in the right direction, something or someone changed the direction I was headed.

Words are always easy to say, but actions are so hard to write into play. I took a sip of the water they provided for us, and looked over at Q again. I wondered what he was thinking. He smiled faintly appearing as nervous as I was. I smiled back just as faint.

The door to the courtroom opened. We both turned and watched as Ahmad came in and took a seat on the back row. Q looked at me, I shrugged my shoulders. I didn't expect him there either. My heart was racing with the possibilities. Who does my heart belong to genuinely and who is merely a want and desire for my life? The questions were playing in my head at the final hour. I could feel the tears coming forth but I pushed them back. I had to remain strong right now. Maybe I should let Q speak first and follow his lead.

"Mr. and Mrs. Robertson, I am so glad to see you back in my courtroom," Judge Michaels began. "Have you been attending marriage counseling as appointed by the court in our last hearing?"

"We have your honor," Q and I spoke in unison.

"Great, was there any progress made in your marriage?"

"There was your honor," we said in unison once again. We were on a roll.

"So are we voiding the divorce papers or moving forward with the proceedings?"

Q looked at me and I him, I glanced back at Ahmad then back at Q. I smiled. My mind was clear; I knew exactly what I needed to do.

JUDGE MICHAELS SLAMMED....

her gavel bringing court to order. Alyssa and I both sat down. She looked over at me at the same time my eyes had made their way to hers. Today, we had to make a decision. Six months ago I knew what that decision was, hell even a few days ago. I love Alyssa, but she keeps pushing and pulling. One day she wants me, the next she doesn't. I'm too damn good of a man to be dangling by a string for any woman and that's including Alyssa.

I took a sip of my water and noticed that she had done the same. It's funny how in sync we are at times. She looked back over at me and for some reason I could detect that she was feeling a little uneasy. I forced a smile to try and calm her down, she smiled back at me but I could tell her heart wasn't in it.

The door to the courtroom opened. We both turned and watched as Gary's ass came strolling in like an invited guest and takes a seat in the back row. This mofo was trying my patience. I looked at Alyssa wondering what the hell was this shit about and she shrugs her shoulders as if her guess was as good as mine. What Gary didn't realize is he just made my decision that much easier. I wasn't trying to deal with him any longer. I didn't trust myself around him, I felt like he would push me to the point of death; for him. Could I just walk away from the woman I love, over some punk ass dude? Not really. Plus, I have to factor in my ego; my walking away gives him the open door.

"Mr. and Mrs. Robertson, I am so glad to see you back in my courtroom," Judge Michaels began. "Have you been attending marriage counseling as appointed by the court in our last hearing?"

"We have your honor," we said together, and I smiled.

"Great, was there any progress made in your marriage?"

"There was your honor," we said at the same time again. Man, we were in sync like a mug.

"So are we voiding the divorce papers or moving forward with the proceedings?"

I looked at Alyssa and watched as she didn't answer before looking over at old dude. Yeah, I knew exactly what I needed to do.